SANTA IN THE SWAMP

SWEET HOME LOUISIANA COZY MYSTERIES
BOOK 2

SUMMER PRESCOTT

SUMMER PRESCOTT BOOKS PUBLISHING

CHAPTER ONE

"Where are you heading, beautiful?" Chas Beckett asked, taking Missy in his arms as she headed for the door, purse in hand.

She lingered a moment, just enjoying the most important person in her world, drinking in the scent of him, her head snuggled against his chest.

"You're going to ruin my hair, mister," she murmured, eyes closed.

"Not a chance, you always look spectacular." Chas chuckled.

With a grin, Missy pulled back. "I'm heading to the grocery store to get some holiday ingredients. I'm in a baking mood."

"I love it when that happens," Chas replied. "Your

baking and cooking are the reasons I'm making one of the spare bedrooms into a gym."

"You have fun with that," Missy said, standing on her tiptoes to kiss him lightly. "And stay out of the kitchen while I'm gone. I'm going to cook up something wonderful for lunch when I get back."

"Yes, ma'am," Chas replied, giving her a mock salute.

When Missy got out of the car in the store parking lot, a chill December breeze made her shiver and pull the tails of her mohair scarf more tightly around her neck. LaChance, Louisiana might not be the coldest spot in the winter, but living in Florida for several years had lessened her tolerance for sub-60's temperatures quite a bit.

Halfway to the grocery store entrance, a movement out of the corner of her eye caught her attention, and Missy turned to see a man sitting with his back against a tree in the vacant lot adjacent to the store. He glanced up, saw her looking in his direction and immediately dropped his gaze.

Missy stood still for a moment, uncertain as to what to do next. The doors to the store slid open and a burst of cheery Christmas music wafted out as laughing shoppers exited.

"It's the season of giving," she said under her

breath. She turned and walked toward the man, who still seemed to be eyeing the grass in front of him.

As she got closer, Missy saw that, though the man's clothes were worn, he looked like he cared about his appearance and seemed clean. He raised his head, his eyes filled with what looked like dread, with a heavy dose of shame. His overgrown hair and beard were white, but the lack of lines on his face made her guess that he might be younger than she was.

"Ma'am, if I'm making you uncomfortable by being here, I'll move along," he said, his tone polite, contrite even.

"I'm not uncomfortable. I just came over to talk to you. Are you okay?" Missy asked, noting that his voice sounded a bit hoarse.

He gave a mirthless chuckle. "I haven't been okay for years, but thanks for asking. Most people don't even look at me anymore, much less ask how I'm doing."

"Are you ill? Or hungry? Is there anything I can do to help you?"

The man's shoulders slumped, and he dropped his gaze again.

"I'm sorry. I didn't mean to offend you," Missy said, her heart aching.

"You didn't, don't worry about that. I just…" he

paused and glanced back up at Missy. "I'm not used to kindness anymore." He shrugged and swallowed hard. "I know I sound funny, but I think I just have a cold. I haven't been to the doctor in years."

"That settles it then. You're going to come into the grocery store with me, and we'll get you some cold medicine and a few other things," Missy said firmly.

The man shook his head. "Thank you, really, but they're not going to let me in there," he said, color rising in his cheeks.

"You wanna bet?" Missy said, cocking one eyebrow. "Come shop with me. It's cold out here and you can get warm for a bit while we pick up a few things. I really love it when someone else pushes the cart for me, if you don't mind."

"Well, if it would help you…" the man replied.

"It surely would," Missy said firmly.

The man rose and dusted off the back of his pants and tattered flannel shirt. "Alright then."

"What's your name?" Missy asked, as he fell into step beside her.

He was shorter than Chas, but then many men were, and had a solid build. If it hadn't been for his lack of grooming and shabby clothing, he'd look like just a regular guy out doing his grocery shopping.

"Dodge. Dodge Leightner," he replied. "I can't remember the last time someone asked me that when it wasn't involved with getting kicked out of a place."

"Nice to meet you, Dodge. I'm Missy, and I can assure you that no one is going to be kicking you out of the grocery store."

"Thank you, ma'am. But I don't have any money," he replied, once again dropping his head, his gaze on the asphalt.

"My treat." Missy smiled.

When Dodge opened his mouth to speak, she interrupted.

"And I think since you don't have a southern accent, you may not know this, but when a southern woman makes up her mind about something, it's best not to cross her." Missy chuckled.

"Yes, ma'am. I got that vibe from you pretty early on," Dodge said, finally smiling.

They strolled into the store together, and Missy nodded at the manager—a young man who was the son of one of her high school classmates. He nodded back, glancing from Missy to Dodge and back again, looking perplexed.

"First things first," Missy said, thinking. "Let's head to the cold medicine aisle and see if we can get you feeling a bit better. Then you'll need some protein, so we'll get some envelopes of tuna and some beef jerky. Do you like both of those?"

Dodge nodded, seemingly stunned.

"Great. You'll need some vitamin C too, so we'll get a bag of oranges. Do you like the big ones or the little ones?" Missy asked.

"I'm not picky," Dodge replied, seeming a bit dazed.

"Good, we'll get the large ones then. We'll also stop by the deli department and get you some ready-made food, and then we'll hit the baking aisle for my holiday supplies."

"Ma'am, you really don't have to do this," Dodge said.

"Of course I don't. But I'm going to, so you'd do well just to come along for the ride," Missy said, not even pausing as she moved toward the medicine aisle.

Dodge pushed the cart, which became more and more loaded down, and followed Missy through the store. They checked out, and Missy asked Dodge to follow her to her car.

He looked confused when she started putting his groceries in the back with hers.

"Don't worry, I'm not taking your dinner away. You're going to come with me to a place where I know you'll be safe and warm for a bit so you can recover from that cold." She reached into her purse and handed him a small packet of tissues. "Here, you might need these."

"You want me to get into your car?" he asked, standing awkwardly behind the grocery cart.

"You bet. It's way too far to walk," Missy replied.

"I don't want to go to jail, ma'am," Dodge whispered.

"I don't want you to either. I told you, I'm taking you someplace safe. Go ahead and put that cart back, then come with me," Missy directed, inclining her head toward the cart bay.

"Are you sure?"

Missy grinned and shook her head. "Go Dodge." She made a shooing motion with her hand. "We have places to be. And quit calling me ma'am, you're making me feel old."

"Okay, ma'am… I mean, Missy," he said, hurrying away with the cart.

Missy got in and started the car. "That poor man," she murmured, watching Dodge walk back, his shoulders hunched against the breeze that had kicked up again.

He hesitated at the passenger door, only opening it when Missy waved him in.

"Where are we going?" he asked, after buckling himself in.

"One of my mother's best friends owns a boarding house here in town."

Dodge's face fell. "I'm sorry, but I wasn't kidding. I really don't have any money."

"I do," Missy said. "And I use it as I please, so don't even try to talk me out of it."

"I'd imagine that'd be a losing proposition." He smiled.

"One hundred percent." Missy laughed.

"Boarding houses still exist?"

"We've got some traditions here in the south that will never go away. Where are you from?"

"Idaho, originally," Dodge replied, a faraway look in his eyes.

"You're a long way from home," Missy commented, pulling into a parking spot in front of a three-story white Victorian house.

"Home isn't even in my vocabulary anymore, Missy."

"Well, we'll just see about that. Come meet Gracie," she said, getting out of the car.

CHAPTER TWO

"Little Melissa!" a spry older woman exclaimed, her hands going to her cheeks when she answered the door and saw Missy on her porch.

The two women embraced for a good long time, and both had tears in their eyes when they parted.

"Please tell me you're back home in LaChance to stay," Gracie said, grasping Missy's hands in her own.

"Yes, ma'am. I'm home." Missy grinned, wiping her eyes. "And it's so good to see you again."

"You are the spittin' image of your sweet mama," Gracie observed, touching Missy's cheek.

She glanced past Missy, still smiling. "Who's your friend?"

"Gracie, this is Dodge. He needs a place to stay, and I bet he'd love some of your homemade chicken broth if you have some handy. He's recovering from a cold. Do you have any rooms?"

"I have a room and a stockpot full of soup simmering in the kitchen right now. Y'all come in and we'll get you settled, Dodge," Gracie said, opening the door wide.

The scent of rich chicken broth made Missy's stomach rumble.

"I can't stay, but I'll come back for a visit soon," she promised.

"Alright, sugar. We've got some catching up to do, so don't you dare be a stranger," Gracie said, giving her a hug. "I'll take good care of your friend here."

"Thank you," Missy said, hugging her mother's best friend fiercely.

Seeing her brought back fond memories of baking together, sharing, and laughing in her mother's kitchen. With a lump in her throat, she headed out to the car to bring in Dodge's groceries, while Gracie showed him to his room.

She set them on the table in the kitchen and slipped out the front door, feeling an ache in her chest. What she wouldn't give to have just a few minutes to be young again. To be carefree in the company of the world's best parents.

"I miss y'all so much," she whispered, a tear slipping down her cheek as she started the engine.

———

Missy had a dusting of flour on her nose and was gazing down at her latest creations when Chas came into the kitchen.

"What do we have here?" he asked, surveying the platter of cupcakes. "I didn't think after the chicken and biscuits you made me for lunch that I'd ever be hungry again, but these look and smell amazing."

"I'm happy with the way that they came out." Missy folded her arms and nodded. "They're chocolate cupcakes, with cream cheese mint cookie filling, chocolate buttercream frosting and a crushed candy cane sprinkled on top. I'm hoping I can unload most of them on Kaylee and Gracie." She grinned.

Before Chas could reply, Missy's phone rang.

"It's Sue Ann," she said, glancing at the screen.

"The realtor?" Chas asked.

Missy nodded and shooed him away as she hit the answer button on her phone. "Hey Sue Ann, how are you?" she asked.

"Fabulous as always." Sue Ann chuckled. "Are y'all settling in well at your haunted mansion?"

"It's not haunted. It's a perfectly lovely house." Missy laughed. "But yes, we're happy here. Still changing some things up a bit, but I'm so glad we chose this place."

"I am, too. I thought that darn thing would never sell," Sue Ann replied. "So anyway, girl, the reason I'm calling is that my realty group is sponsoring a Holiday Gala that will benefit a local homeless shelter. I thought you and Chas might want to come and write a big, fat check."

"Don't be shy, Sue Ann, tell me how you really feel." Missy chuckled. "Of course we'll come. Just send me an evite with the details."

"Oh honey, you two will literally get an engraved invitation, and I'll drop it off this afternoon, since it's in a couple of days. Sorry for the late notice, I'm just getting over a vicious cold, so I'm making about a thousand phone calls today. It's going to be at the wedding venue that's in the old Dellville Mansion ballroom."

"Oh, I love that place!" Missy exclaimed. "I went to a cotillion there once."

"Of course you do. It's ancient and draped with Spanish moss, it's right up your alley," Sue Ann teased.

"You know it. What's the theme for the gala?"

Missy asked, already planning to go shopping for something to wear.

"Santa Claus is coming to town. We held a toy drive, so Santa will be there to give away the toys to some of the kids in the community who wouldn't have any Christmas gifts otherwise."

Missy bit her lip. "Oh, that's precious, Sue Ann, I love it."

"There's only one problem." Sue Ann sighed.

"Oh?"

"Yeah, our Santa got called out of the country on business and won't be back in time for the gala, so now we won't have one. We may have to wrap your hunky hubby in pillows, give him a fake beard and mustache and spray his hair white. Think he'd be up for it?"

"Maybe, but I think I actually might have a better option. Reserve two tickets for us, send me the details, and I'll get back to you about Santa," Missy promised.

"What do you have up your sleeve now, Melissa Beckett?" Sue Ann asked.

"You'll see. I'll be in touch."

"Hey, Gracie. Is Dodge around?" Missy asked, following her mother's friend into the boarding house. When she learned of Sue Ann's plight, she'd wasted no time in setting out to secure a Santa Claus, showing up at Gracie's the very next morning.

"Yes, he is, and he's such a nice man. He helps out with yard work and kitchen clean up. It's like having a husband around without any of the fuss that comes along with that." Gracie chuckled.

"Oh, good. I'm glad it's working out," Missy replied, relieved. "Just let me know what your rates are these days, and I'll write you a check."

"Honey, don't even think about it. I'm glad to help him get back on his feet. I gave him some of Herb's old clothes that I couldn't bear to get rid of after he passed, and it seemed to make him feel a bit better about things."

"That's great to hear. Is he in his room?" Missy asked.

"Heavens no. That man is almost never in his room. He's always puttering with something. Right now, he's out back in the shed cleaning the blades on my lawn mower since we won't be mowing for a few months. Go on out and have a visit. I think you'll be able to see a bit of a spark in him that wasn't there when he first arrived."

"That's wonderful. Thanks, Gracie."

Missy went out the back door and headed for the shed, where she saw Dodge using what looked like a piece of black sandpaper to clean and sharpen the blades.

"Hey, Dodge!" she called out, striding toward him.

"Missy, nice to see you," he said, his voice showing none of the hoarseness that it had when she'd dropped him off at Gracie's.

"You, too. It sounds like your cold is gone."

"Yeah, Gracie's soup is magical." He smiled. Missy noticed that his teeth were clean and looked healthy.

"Gracie herself is magical. She was like a second mom to me back in the day."

"Lucky you." Dodge nodded.

"Definitely. Hey, I've got a question for you. A friend of mine is in a bit of a jam, and I'm hoping that you might be able to help her out?"

"I'd be happy to help if I'm able. What's going on?"

"Her company is sponsoring a gala that will help fund Second Start shelter. They're giving away toys to kids in need, but their Santa got called out of the country on business, and since you have the hair and beard for it, I thought you might be interested in doing it," Missy explained.

Dodge's face had darkened the moment she'd mentioned Second Start, and he shook his head.

"After all you and Gracie have done for me, I really hate to refuse. But I'm sorry, I can't support something that benefits that place," he said quietly, a new dignity in his tone.

"Oh? Why?" Missy frowned.

"The owner of it treats people like… like they aren't even human. It's disgusting." Dodge shook his head.

"Did you have a bad interaction with him?" Missy asked quietly.

"If you consider being left in the rain because I pointed out a chair with a broken spring that sliced open a teenager's leg, then yeah, I guess you could say we had a bad interaction." A muscle in his jaw flexed.

"That's awful. What happened to the teenager?" Missy asked, aghast.

"Don't know for sure, but I heard that Feeney had the night watchman give him some gauze and fifty bucks to keep his mouth shut."

"Feeney?" Missy frowned.

"The owner. He's a real piece of work. Pretends to

be all pious and concerned, until the donors leave the building."

"Well, maybe if we have a chance to talk to him, we can change that," Missy mused. "Anyway, my thought is that it's so hard this time of year for kids who are in need. It would be lovely if you could be there for them," she said softly.

"Yeah, I suppose you're right. There's no reason that his lack of character should deprive the kids from seeing Santa." Dodge nodded.

"So, you'll do it?" Missy asked.

"Yeah, I'll do it," he agreed.

"That's wonderful! Thank you so much." Missy grinned. "And since you're going to be Santa, there's someplace we need to go."

"There is?"

"Yep, think of it as the North Pole for adults. Do you want to go now?" Missy asked.

"Umm, sure. I can finish this up later," Dodge replied, wiping his hands on a shop rag.

"I'll just have some tea with Gracie and wait if you want to wash up a bit first."

"Sounds good."

"So where are we going?" Dodge asked as Missy pulled out onto the street.

"The mall."

"The mall? Why?"

"Because Santa is going to have his beard and hair tamed, and please don't take this the wrong way, because Gracie was wonderful to give you some clothes, but something from this century would be nice. So, while I shop for a dress for the gala, you can pick up some things to wear," Missy replied.

"But my situation hasn't changed financially," he said, staring out the window.

"Think of the clothes and haircut as compensation for playing Santa at the party."

"But I'm doing that for the kids. I don't want to receive anything from it."

"I know you don't, and that's why you'll be a perfect Santa. But trust me on this, the right outfit can make you feel better about yourself, and it's high time that you did, don't you think?"

"I don't deserve it." Dodge stared down at his hands.

"No one deserves the life you've had to lead and the treatment you've received from people who think they're better than you are. They're not. They shouldn't think they are, and you shouldn't either."

Dodge swallowed hard and nodded. "I guess."

"Good, then it's settled, and here we are," Missy said, as she turned into the mall parking lot.

The barbershop in the mall was full service and Missy insisted that Dodge receive premium service. His hair and beard were washed with a special purple shampoo that smelled like apples. It gave the already white hair a Santa sparkle. Then he had a facial, followed by a hair and beard trim. When he walked back out into the waiting area, Missy's mouth fell open in delight.

"You look amazing, Dodge! How do you feel? Have you seen yourself yet?"

Dodge shook his head. "I don't look in mirrors," he said quietly.

Missy looked him right in the eye and spoke, her voice gentle but firm. "You need to see who you are, Dodge. The man who has been shoved into the background because of his situation shows on your face now. You're a good person and you need to look yourself in the eye and realize it," she said softly.

The barber folded his arms and nodded at Dodge. "Ain't nothin' to be ashamed of, man."

He led Dodge over to one of the mirrors and placed him directly in front of it.

"Why don't you check out my hard work," he

prompted.

Fists clenched at his sides, Dodge raised his gaze and met his own eyes in the mirror. A sound came out of him, part surprise, part raw, guttural emotion. His eyes welled with tears, as did Missy's while she watched him carefully examine his own face as if seeing it for the first time.

"You matter, man. You're a person, just like everybody else," the barber said, clapping him on the back.

Dodge nodded, his mouth working as he seemed to try desperately to cling to his composure.

"That's you," Missy said. "And tomorrow night, that's Santa." She smiled.

Dodge smiled faintly at that.

Missy tried to hand the barber her credit card and he shook his head. "Sorry ma'am, it's store policy that we don't charge Santa."

"Thank you," Missy whispered, tucking her card away. "Dodge, are you ready to go?" she asked.

"Yeah, I am," he said, finally seeming to be at peace with his new image. "No idea how I got so old though. White hair? How did that happen?" He smiled.

"Happens to the best of us." Missy chuckled. "Let's go shopping."

As they made their way to Missy's favorite department store in the mall, small children would either stare at him when they passed or would run up to him and wrap themselves around his knees shouting, "Santa!!"

Dodge rose to the occasion well, smiling, patting them on the head and telling them to be good boys and girls.

"Somehow I think the role of Santa is going to come pretty naturally to you," Missy teased. "Now, this is my favorite store. I'm heading to the dress department. I want you to pick out at least three pairs of pants and five or six shirts along with all the basics—socks, underwear, etc… and a good winter coat. I'll meet you in the men's department after I've found a dress."

"You've already done so much for me. I can't…" he began, his face flushing.

"You can, and you will. You just brought such joy to those kids. I want to do the same for you, so quit trying to get out of it and go get some clothes, young man," Missy said with mock sternness.

Dodge took in a big breath and blew it out. "Alright. I'll try," he said, looking as though he'd been asked to crawl through a pit of poisonous snakes.

"I have confidence in you," Missy teased. "See you soon."

She had flipped through the rack of formal dresses and was almost to the end when she saw a gown that took her breath away. It was a red satin beaded dress with a floor length skirt that looked like it had been formed from poinsettia leaves. It had spaghetti straps, a sweetheart neckline, and a low-cut back that was more daring than she would normally wear. She looked at the tag and saw that it was her size.

"I have to try this on," she murmured, reaching for the hanger.

When she put it on, it just felt right. She looked at her reflection in the mirror and her eyes welled with tears. "I look young again," she whispered, smoothing her hands over the silken fabric.

She stepped out of the dressing room to gaze at the dress in the three-way mirror that was just outside the door.

"Oh wow, that is stunning," a twenty-something salesperson commented.

"This dress is everything," Missy breathed.

"And you look fabulous in it. You know what would make it look even better?" the young woman asked.

Missy's heart sank. "A twenty-year-old body?"

she tried to laugh.

"No! You rock that dress, don't take it like that. I was just going to say that there's a gorgeous pair of red crystal shoes in the shoe department that will be the icing on the cake. You seriously have to get that dress. The way it looks on you is exactly the way it's supposed to look." She smiled.

"Thank you." A blush rose from Missy's neck and didn't stop until it heated the tips of her ears. "I'll take it, and then I'll go try on the shoes." She couldn't wait to see Chas's reaction to the dress.

Minutes later, with shoes, the dress, and a new bottle of perfume in hand, Missy headed for the men's department to find Dodge. She saw him sitting in a chair beside the dressing rooms looking uncomfortable.

"Did you find some things?" she asked.

"Yeah, a salesguy came over and helped me. I tried everything on and it worked out." Dodge nodded.

"How did it feel? Did you look at yourself in the mirror?"

He stood. "I did. It felt strange, almost like I was normal again."

"I suspect you've always been normal, but you believed people when they treated you strangely,"

Missy replied. "Let's buy those things, then we'll get you over to the shoe department. I would've forgotten about that part, but I remembered when I got a pair for myself."

After purchasing his new clothing and selecting a pair of running shoes, casual loafers, and a pair of black winter boots to wear with his Santa costume that would be provided by Sue Ann, they headed out of the mall.

"You know, now that I think about it, I don't believe that I'll be comfortable at all around those fancy people who will be at the gala," Dodge confessed.

"Don't worry about it. My friend Sue Ann is coordinating it and she's very nice. My husband Chas and I will be there, and you'll be surrounded by giggling kids most of the time anyway. That'll lift your spirits for sure," Missy reassured him.

"Yeah, I guess that's true. Maybe this will be good for me. I want a chance to prove that I can be brave and that I haven't given up on myself," Dodge said quietly.

"Absolutely. Now is your chance, and I know you're going to be great."

"I sure hope so." He sighed and stared out of the window.

CHAPTER THREE

"I bought you a cummerbund to go with your tux. It matches my dress and I put it on top of the island in your closet," Missy called out as she stood in her closet zipping up her dress.

"Wow, red satin?" Chas's voice sounded a million miles away, though his closet shared a wall with hers. "I can't wait to see your dress."

"Well, you're going to have to, mister. I still have to touch up my makeup and put up my hair," Missy said.

She went to her vanity and sat down, putting on another light touch of blush and giving her lips a wonderfully pouty look with lipstick in a shade that nearly exactly matched her gown. "That's gonna drive him crazy," she murmured, checking her reflection to make sure everything was okay. Once her makeup passed inspection, she took her hair out of the hot rollers that she'd put in before getting dressed and pinned it up into an elaborate updo with a cascade of curls. She wore a diamond necklace and earring set that Chas had given her a couple of decades prior and slipped her feet into the exquisite crystal encrusted shoes, feeling very much like an impostor.

"I'm just a cupcake baker from small-town Louisiana," she told the mirror.

"No, you're the most beautiful girl in the world," Chas said, appearing in the doorway looking positively debonaire in his tux. His eyes were warm and Missy wondered how on earth she'd gotten so lucky in life.

"You're too kind, darlin'," Missy said, smiling at him in the mirror.

"Nope, I'm just telling the truth." He came in and bent down to kiss her bare shoulder. "You get more beautiful every day, and don't even try to tell me that you're not using that red lipstick to keep me spell-bound all evening." He smiled.

"Guilty," Missy said, with a sly grin. "Are you about ready to go?"

"Ready whenever you are, love."

Heads turned when Missy and Chas entered the

ballroom. Missy of course thought that it was just because Chas was so entirely handsome in his tuxedo. She immediately spotted Dodge in his Santa suit, sitting in an oversized chair by the Christmas tree that dominated one end of the ballroom. The tree was surrounded by stacks of gifts with names on them for the children who would be attending.

Sue Ann seemed to be giving Dodge instructions, so Missy told Chas to come with her to say hi to them.

"Well, if you two don't look like the holiday edition of Vogue magazine!" Sue Ann exclaimed, hands on hips, eyebrows raised. Her brilliant red hair had been swept back into a chic chignon, and her sequined dress was the delicate color of pink champagne.

She and Missy carefully embraced with air kisses so that dresses weren't snagged and lipstick wasn't smudged, then Sue Ann greeted Chas similarly, with a, "Hiya handsome."

"Dodge, you look right at home in that Santa suit," Missy said.

His eyes actually twinkled. "I may have found my new career," he joked.

Chas joined Missy and she introduced them, then left them to chat while Sue Ann introduced her to some of the other guests. Some of them were people whom Missy hadn't seen in years, others were either newcomers, or people from out of town.

"I'm dying of thirst—want to get some punch?" Missy asked Sue Ann after a couple from New Orleans moved on.

"You read my mind," Sue Ann replied.

A beady-eyed, balding man with a paunchy stomach, who had a gum-chewing blonde's hand tucked into the crook of his arm intercepted them on their way to the punchbowl.

"Good turn out tonight, little Susie," he said to Sue Ann in an impossibly patronizing tone. Missy could practically see her friend's teeth being set on edge.

"Thanks, Feeney," Sue Ann replied, her eyelid twitching slightly. "Who's your lovely companion?" she asked, in a syrupy tone that alerted Missy to the fact that the realtor was ready and willing to put their host, Feeney Finklesworth, in his place if necessary.

"May I present Shalimar Dryden. Honey, this here is Sue Ann, who put together this little shindig," Feeney said.

"Pleasure." Sue Ann nodded when Shalimar left her hand firmly fastened on the place where Feeney's bicep, if he had one, would have been. "Feeney

Finklesworth, my dear friend Melissa Beckett," she said, introducing Missy.

Feeney reached for Missy's hand and brought it to his lips, lingering a shade too long for Missy's comfort level.

"Enchante, Melissa," Feeney said, looking at Missy like she was the crispiest piece of fried chicken in the bucket.

"Nice to meet you," Missy said coolly, then turned to his date. "Shalimar, what a lovely name. My aunt, Emilie, used to wear that perfume."

"What perfume? I'm not wearing any perfume, just some coconut body spray." Shalimar frowned.

Missy and Sue Ann exchanged a glance.

"Shalimar was a perfume that was really popular a few years ago," Missy said kindly.

"Oh. Never heard of it." Shalimar shrugged.

"Well, it was lovely to chat with both of you, ladies, but if you'll excuse us, I need to prepare to make this evening even more special." Feeney glanced at Shalimar, who seemed to be focusing on something over Missy's left shoulder and waggled his eyebrows in a most distasteful manner.

Missy's brows rose and she looked at Sue Ann, whose expression was a reflection of her own.

"Wow," Missy said. "I see now why Dodge isn't terribly fond of that man."

"Yeah, you've gotta be pretty awful to get on Santa's bad side." Sue Ann nodded. "Speaking of Santa, who is adorable by the way, let's bring him some punch too. The kids will be here in a few minutes."

Dodge had barely finished his cup of punch before a hoard of excited children came into the ballroom, wide-eyed with wonder. He did an amazing job of making each child feel special, and their eyes lit up when he handed them gifts that had been selected just for them, along with a small sack of brightly colored candies.

Once the kids left the ballroom, chattering and laughing, the adults seemed merrier as well. Except one.

Missy saw Shalimar rushing toward the kitchen with a look of abject fury on her face.

"Chas, look," she whispered, nudging him with her elbow. "That's Feeney's girlfriend. She seems angry."

"I'd likely be angry too if I had to put up with Feeney," he commented mildly, having met the insufferable man earlier. "I don't see Dodge, do you?"

Missy scanned the room. Santa's chair was empty,

and she didn't see any sign of Dodge. "He's probably overwhelmed, poor guy. Must be catching his breath somewhere."

"Well, if it isn't Melissa Gladstone." Missy heard a vaguely familiar voice say. She turned toward it and saw a fashionably thin woman in heavy makeup smiling at her.

"Penelope?" Missy gasped. "Girl, I haven't seen you in decades. How are you?" she asked her former classmate.

"I can't complain," Penny replied, turning her gaze to Chas. "And who do we have here?" she purred, her gaze taking him in from head to toe.

"This is my husband, Chas. Chas, this is Penelope. We went to school together," Missy introduced them.

"Pleased to meet you, Penelope," Chas said, shaking her hand. "Or is it Penny?"

"The last time someone called me Penny they found themselves in the middle of a nasty little audit," Penelope replied.

"Noted." Chas chuckled.

"So, are you involved with Second Start?" Missy asked.

Penelope made a face. "If you consider being the ex-wife of the owner, I suppose I am."

"You and... Feeney?" Missy's brows rose.

"I know, hard to believe, right? We divorced last year, and I'm much happier with my cats and money than I ever was with that foul man." Penelope pursed her lips as though she'd just caught a whiff of something awful. "Where is he anyway?" she asked, scanning the clusters of people in the ballroom.

"Well, I could be wrong," Missy said in a low voice, leaning in. "But I'm guessing he may be somewhere having a conversation with his date. She stormed out of here not too long ago looking very angry."

"Hmpf... Perhaps that's what he gets when he finds his dates at a bowling alley," Penelope scoffed.

Before Missy could respond, they heard a loud shout from the direction of the kitchen. "Someone call the police!"

CHAPTER FOUR

While most of the group stood frozen in alarm, Missy's instincts kicked in and she immediately rushed toward the kitchen with Chas at her heels.

There were people huddled near the exit at the back of the kitchen and Missy wove through them like a knife through butter. When she stepped out onto the back stoop, the sight that met her eyes left her horrified. Dodge sat on the bottom step, his head in his hands. Not even four feet in front of him on the asphalt behind the mansion, the motionless form of Feeney Finklesworth was sprawled in a manner that left no doubt as to his condition.

Missy hurried down the steps and immediately smelled the overwhelming odor of alcohol when she leaned down to speak to Dodge.

"Hey, are you okay? What happened?" she whispered.

"I don't… I don't know. I'm so dizzy," Dodge mumbled, his words seeming garbled.

"Dodge, were you drinking?" Missy frowned.

He shook his head and listed to the left, catching the railing to keep from falling over.

Missy's heart sunk. If Dodge had hoped to make this evening a good start to his new life, it appeared as though he'd botched it. Perhaps fatally.

"Look out, coming through. I'm a doctor."

A tall, thin woman in a turquoise gown brushed past Missy, glancing at Dodge, but continuing on her way to Feeney. She felt for a pulse and shook her head.

"Folks, there's nothing we can do. Maybe you should all just go back inside," she said, standing slowly as the first four police cars pulled up, lights and sirens blazing.

Two policemen stood near Feeney after conferring with the doctor who then went back inside, and another officer pointed at Dodge and told him not to move.

"That tone isn't necessary," Missy muttered, shivering. It was cold outside, her adrenaline levels were astronomical, and she wasn't dressed for the outdoors.

Dodge shook his head and winced. "I have no idea what happened."

"Well, that's not hard to believe, pal. You smell like a brewery," one of the police officers commented, a scowl on his face.

"I don't drink, man. Not at all," Dodge protested, going pale.

"It's okay, Dodge. We'll get this figured out," Missy said, rubbing her upper arms to warm them.

"Ma'am, I'm going to need you to go back inside while we secure the scene," the officer who had given Dodge a dirty look decreed.

"Fine." She patted Dodge on the shoulder and turned to go, something on the inner curl of the top of the wrought iron stair rail catching her eye. A scrap of fabric. She also spotted Dodge's Santa hat on the stoop and when she bent to pick it up, she slid her cellphone out of her evening bag and snapped a picture of the fabric.

The hat had a spot of blood spoiling the fluffy white of its brim, and when Missy looked at the back of Dodge's neck, she noticed a bit of blood seeping through his pristine white curls.

"Lady, I'm not going to tell you again. This is an active investigation, and you need to go inside."

"Well, there's no need to be rude about it," Missy

snapped. "When you're done berating people, maybe you could get Santa some medical help."

She turned and went inside with Chas. Dodge's eyes when she left were glassy and bewildered.

CHAPTER FIVE

Missy beat the batter for her crepes perhaps a bit harder than was absolutely necessary. She was making breakfast for Kaylee and Chas, but her mind was on the gala and the events that unfolded at the end of it.

Kaylee entered the kitchen wearing leggings and a sweater that reached nearly to her knees. She'd said that on her day off, she fully intended to be warm and comfortable.

"Your Santa is in jail," she announced, easing onto a barstool at the kitchen island.

Missy's whisk clanged against the side of the glass bowl, and she turned to face her daughter.

"For what?" she gasped, brows raised.

"Murder."

"I can't believe it." Missy shook her head.

"Yeah, he seems like a nice guy. Unfortunately, he says he can't remember anything other than going out for some air, then waking up with a headache next to a body," Kaylee replied.

"He must've been hit from behind because his head was bleeding and there was blood on the Santa hat," Missy mused, pouring a puddle of batter onto a sizzling skillet.

"Or he could've hit his head because he passed out from drinking too much," Kaylee said.

"Did he do a breathalyzer test?" Missy asked, expertly flipping the crepe.

"No. He was taken to the hospital for a concussion. And before you ask, they did blood work, but the tox results haven't come in yet."

"Who else have they talked to and how do they know that it was murder?" Missy asked.

"I'm not sure." Kaylee shrugged. "I'm not on the case, but I doubt they talked to anyone else because they have a suspect in custody."

"That's just crazy. Feeney's date left in a huff, and his ex-wife had nothing good to say about him, but they homed in on someone who was there to make children happy for the holidays." Missy made a face and transferred the crepe to a platter before pouring another one. "Now, the ex-wife would never do something like commit murder, she'd be worried that she might break a nail, but the victim wasn't even close to being a well-liked man."

"Mom, I know you always want to save the world, but I'm telling you, don't get involved," Kaylee insisted.

Missy turned and pointed her spatula at her daughter. "Darlin' that's like telling me not to breathe.

CHAPTER SIX

"Should I be worried?" Chas asked when he walked into the kitchen and saw Missy pulling two dozen cupcakes out of the oven.

"You know me by now, what do you think?" Missy gave him a look and set the pans on cooling racks.

"I think sometimes that tender heart and feisty attitude of yours gets you into trouble," Chas replied, brushing a dusting of flour from her nose and kissing her forehead.

"You know I'm not one to let injustice happen," Missy said, taking off her oven mitts and tossing them into a drawer.

"I know, that's why I just ask you to be careful

and keep me informed." Chas brushed a curl from her forehead.

"I'm taking sympathy cupcakes to Feeney's girl-friend," Missy admitted.

"So that you can try to figure out if she killed her boyfriend for some reason," Chas added. "It never ceases to amaze me that you have no qualms whatso-ever about keeping company with potential murderers."

"Well, somebody has to. The police certainly aren't." Missy made a face.

"Got your pepper spray?" Chas asked.

"Darn tootin' I do. Besides, she's a tiny little thing. I'm sure I could take her down if I had to." Missy grinned.

"I'm just glad we're on the same side." Chas chuckled, drawing her into his arms.

Missy drove to a part of LaChance that she'd never been to before. The houses were small and most were in need of repair or paint. The yards were filled with autumn leaves and children's toys. Except for Shali-mar's yard. It stood out in its austerity. There was no fence around it, and it was completely devoid of bushes, leaves, or personality. It was an empty canvas that desperately needed pots of flowers or something decorative to show that someone lived there. It was clean, but bare, in a way that made it seem defensive rather than abandoned. Missy would've placed a bet that there was no welcome mat on the porch in front of the pristinely clean grey door.

She took the pink box that she'd filled with holiday themed cupcakes and marched up to that grey door, knocking on it because there was no doorbell.

A tired-looking blonde opened it and said, "Yeah?"

If Missy hadn't recognized her nasally-tinged voice, she would've sworn that it wasn't Shalimar. With her hair pulled back, dark circles under her puffy eyes, and no makeup, she looked very different than when she'd been squired around the ballroom on Feeney's arm.

"Uh, hi. I met you last night. I'm Melissa," Missy said, hoping for a glimmer of recognition.

"I met a lot of people last night." Shalimar sighed.

"Well, after what happened, I just wanted to come over and see if you're okay."

"Do I look okay to you?" Shalimar folded her arms and stared at Missy.

Missy held up the pink box. "I brought you some cupcakes."

Shalimar stared at the box for a moment, then took it. "I don't usually eat dessert, but I starved for a week to fit into that dress. You wanna come in?" she asked, opening the cover and selecting a cupcake.

"Sure. Yeah, I'd like that," Missy said, watching Shalimar take a massive bite out of a vanilla caramel cupcake.

The inside of the small house was just as plain as the outside and just as clean, with white walls, a few tasteful pieces of thrift shop furniture and absolutely no décor. Missy sat on the edge of a plain brown couch while Shalimar curled up in an overstuffed plaid chair. A fat orange tabby strutted into the living room and jumped up onto Shalimar's lap, settling in next to the box of cupcakes.

"Feeney hated cats," she said, her mouth full of cake, frosting, and caramel.

"Did you two date for a long time?" Missy asked.

Shalimar sighed. "Since shortly after his divorce." She tossed the empty wrapper back into the box and plucked out a strawberry cheesecake cupcake. "I was mad at him last night, but I definitely didn't want things to end like that for him." She took a huge bite.

"Lots of couples have tension during the holidays

for some reason," Missy commented, staring at Shalimar as she ate the cupcake in huge gulps.

"I bet you and your hottie don't," she spoke through a mouthful of frosting and cake, making her words sound mushy.

"Well, we've been together for many years," Missy said carefully, not wanting to offend her.

"Yeah, lots of people fight during the holidays, but I bet it's not because they got a proposal with a fake diamond ring from someone who could more than afford the real thing." The bitterness in her tone wasn't muted by a barrier of cupcake. "I can spot a fake a mile away and with all the money that Feeney has, he could've at least gotten me a real ring," she continued, swallowing the last bite of strawberry cheesecake and selecting a chocolate mocha mint from the box. "He said it was temporary while my real one was being made, but I didn't believe him."

Shalimar paused, chewing slowly and staring into space.

"But if you loved him, did it really matter if the diamond was real or not?" Missy asked, almost feeling sorry for Feeney. Almost.

"Easy for you to say," Shalimar scoffed. "I see that rock on your finger. If you fall into the pool, you'd sink straight to the bottom." She shook her head. "Love? I don't know about all that, but I know that Feeney was my ticket out of this dump. I could marry him and never have to work again. A girl can put up with a lot for that kind of life."

Missy blinked, hoping her reaction didn't show on her face.

"Oh, I don't know," she managed finally as Shalimar popped the last bite of chocolate mocha mint into her mouth and reached for a sugarplum fairy cupcake. "A marriage *with* love can be tough, but love gets you through. I can't imagine a marriage without love."

Shalimar rolled her eyes. "Of course you can't imagine it, you've got both. Now that Feeney's dead, I'm looking at working double shifts at the LaChance Lucky Lanes. Hopefully I'm in his will. We were together long enough, and he proposed, so hopefully he took care of business before he kicked it," she mused.

Suddenly, Shalimar froze, the sugarplum fairy cupcake halfway to her mouth. The color drained from her face, leaving her skin a sickly pale green. She threw the cupcake back into the box and stood quickly, dislodging the cat from her lap with a cranky mew of protest.

"You gotta go. I'm going to be sick," she said, darting down the hall.

"Do you need help?" Missy called out, hearing the gut-wrenching sounds of retching after the slam of the bathroom door.

When she got no answer, she reached down to pet the cat, who was insistently bonking his head against her shin, before rising and heading for the door.

CHAPTER SEVEN

Feeling a bit nauseated herself, after overhearing Shalimar's unfortunate situation, Missy decided to take her mind off her stomach by stopping at the police station to check on Dodge.

The desk sergeant gazed at her suspiciously when she stepped up to the counter.

"Help you?" the woman who was built like a fire-plug asked, sounding like the least helpful person on the planet.

"Yes, I'm here to bail out Dodge Leightner," she said on impulse.

"Can't. Judge hasn't set his bail yet. Being in the hospital delayed the process."

"For how long?" Missy asked.

"Long as it takes." The sergeant stared at her.

"Of course, why didn't I think of that?" Missy shot back, then took a breath. "Okay, fine, can I at least visit with him for a bit?"

"No ma'am."

Missy's eyes narrowed, and the sergeant leaned forward.

"Look, lady. You've already got a reputation as a troublemaker around here. I suggest you find a different hobby and let us do the police work."

Missy felt a burning in the pit of her stomach that had nothing to do with nausea and she leaned in, nearly nose to nose with the sergeant.

"I suggest that y'all start doing your jobs so that law abiding citizens don't end up sitting in jail. If you did, I wouldn't have to," she said with a saccharin smile that bared her teeth just a bit.

The sergeant's face flushed a violent red and she stepped back away from the desk as Missy turned and strode toward the door.

Missy stopped, her hand on the handle to exit, and turned around. "By the way, the best way to get me to do something is to tell me not to. Have a lovely day."

Missy fumed all the way home. It wasn't just the rude sergeant, it was the fact that she felt helpless, and even though Dodge had reeked of alcohol, she was convinced he was innocent.

When she pulled into the driveway, Percy, the wonderful older man who had taken care of their historical home long before Missy lived in it, was hanging Christmas lights and decorations. Missy sat in the car for a moment just taking it all in. She drew in a deep breath and slowly let it out, trying to breathe away some of the stress of her day so far.

"This season is about giving and helping," she murmured, her breath catching when Percy tested the lights and turned the outside of the house into a fairy-land even in the middle of the afternoon. "I'm going to get Santa out of jail. Somehow, some way, I'm going to prove he's innocent," she vowed.

"Percy, you've outdone yourself," she called up to him, while he stood on a ladder hanging a massive, fully lit snowflake.

"Oh ma'am, this here ain't nothin'." He grinned broadly. "Just you wait and see what it looks like when I get done."

"I can't wait," Missy said, with a smile of relief. Sometimes she just needed a reminder of all the good in the world so that she could keep beating back the not-so-good. Percy nodded, his face glowing with pride.

"It'll be ready tonight, ma'am," he promised.

Missy went into the house and rolled up her sleeves, ready to do some serious baking.

"After what I saw Shalimar do with those cupcakes, I think I'm going to bake some cookies this time," she muttered, grabbing ingredients from the pantry.

After she slid the first batch of traditional sugar cookies into the oven and set the timer, she pulled out her laptop. "Okay, let's learn a little bit more about Dodge Leightner before I go completely out on a limb for him," she mused, scrolling and clicking.

She discovered an old story featuring him and immediately became engrossed.

"Oh, Dodge." She sighed, tears welling in her eyes. Skimming the article, she read key facts aloud, his tale growing more tragic by the moment.

"You're a veteran. You had a wife who died in childbirth and you raised a daughter on your own. Let me see if I can find her."

Missy searched the little girl's name, Anna, with Dodge's last name, and couldn't find any information about her. "You must've gotten married, Anna. I wonder, was your daddy there?"

She clicked back onto the search page and found another, more recent, but still older article. Dodge had retired from the military and was working for a major corporation until he was downsized. According to the bankruptcy records that Missy found, he lost his house and everything he owned. There were no more pictures of him with his daughter after that.

"That poor man," she mused. "He's had such a rough life."

"Who did?" Chas asked, coming into the kitchen. "I smelled cookies and figured that something must be wrong. Are you sad about Santa?"

"Sad, frustrated, all kinds of things. I just find it difficult to believe that he's done this awful thing. He's had a hard life, but he seems like a decent person," Missy replied.

"Sweetie, I love you and your kind heart, but for all we know, Dodge could be dangerous. You need to let the police handle this."

Missy closed her laptop and tossed some powdered sugar into a bowl to start her homemade cookie frosting. "You talked to him for quite a while at the gala, did he strike you as a murderer?" she challenged.

"No, he didn't, but we don't know what he's been through and what his experiences may have done to his judgment," Chas said gently.

"I'm sorry, but I just don't buy it. He's not a killer, Chas, I feel that in my bones." Missy shook her head. "Something's wrong here, and I just can't turn my back on a human being who has no resources."

Chas nodded. "I'll have Spencer look into it. He wanted to let us know his big news when Kaylee was here too, so I invited both of them to dinner tonight."

Missy grinned. "Finally! He wouldn't tell me what it is, and I've been badgering him since he arrived."

Chas laughed. "Well, to be fair, we've been so busy getting ready for the holidays, and he's been busy too, that we haven't really had the chance for a good get-together. We have some catching up to do."

"I know. I missed that boy so much. What's he been up to while he's been here anyway? I've hardly seen him."

Chas shrugged. "Your guess is as good as mine. I haven't had any secret conversations with him if that's what you're wondering."

Missy pointed her stirring spoon at him. "You'd better not be keeping secrets, mister," she said playfully. "Oh, my goodness, I need to come up with a plan for dinner," she gasped.

"No, you don't. I booked Le Soir for us. All you have to do is look pretty and give hugs."

"That I can do," Missy replied snuggling into him.

"Yes, you can my love."

CHAPTER EIGHT

"Hey, Sporty Spice!" Spencer greeted Kaylee by picking her up and swinging her in a circle.

"No one calls me that anymore, 007," Kaylee replied, hugging him back.

"Wow, that's one I haven't heard since you went off to college." Spencer laughed and set her down.

The maître d at Le Soir watched the interaction with a raised eyebrow and a slight smile. Missy, Chas, Spencer, and Kaylee had all arrived at the same time, and their reunion was likely more boisterous than the highbrow crowd at the renowned French restaurant was accustomed to.

"Follow me, please," he said, with a patient smile, once they'd settled down a bit.

He led them to a corner booth that was dimly lit and upholstered in crushed black velvet. Candlelight glimmered on the table, making the crystal glasses sparkle.

"I knew this would be a great place to wear my new dress," Kaylee remarked, as the maître d placed her napkin on her lap.

"You look gorgeous, honey," Missy said. "That blue brings out your eyes."

"I have a new tie," Spencer said, making fun of them.

"Good. I'll have a way to take you down if you pick me up again," Kaylee teased.

"Okay y'all, I've been waiting since Spencer first walked in the door at home. What's your big news?" Missy said, staring him down.

"Sweetie, at least wait until the champagne arrives," Chas said, kissing her cheek.

She turned to regard him with suspicion. "Do you already know?"

Chas held up his hands. "I have no idea, I swear."

Their server approached and took the order for appetizers and champagne, which took merely minutes to deliver. Missy was practically bouncing in her chair, waiting for the meticulous ritual of the tasting and pouring of the champagne to be complete.

When everyone had their glass, and the sommelier left the table, Spencer raised his champagne and said, "I'd like to propose a toast."

Missy's heart skipped a beat. Spencer's face was aglow, so the news had to be something wonderful. Life-changing maybe.

"Here's to new life," he said.

Crystal clinked against crystal and everyone sipped a deliciously fruity champagne.

"Now young man, stop being mysterious. You said a new life, you're not leaving Beckett Enterprises, are you?" Missy gasped, the possibility just dawning on her.

Spencer chuckled. "No, definitely not, but I'm going to need a schedule that has less travel and less time away from home."

Missy paled. "Oh, honey, are you sick?" Her stomach sank.

He laughed. "No, I'm not but Izzy is. They tell us it'll go away in three to six months."

Missy shook her head. "See, y'all should have listened to me. I knew you'd catch something when you went on that eco trip in the jungle without electricity."

Kaylee and Chas burst into laughter and Chas rose

to hug Spencer. "Congratulations, son," he said, positively beaming.

Missy was befuddled.

"Mama, Spencer and Izzy are having a baby," Kaylee explained, moving in for her turn at a hug.

"Oh, Spencer! I'm gonna be a grandma??" She burst into tears.

"Ye,s ma'am," he said, engulfing her in a bear hug.

Their salads arrived and they settled back into the booth. Chas stood, raised his glass, and tapped it with his spoon, catching the attention of other diners. "Ladies and gentlemen, I'm thrilled to announce that my lovely wife and I are about to become grandparents for the first time."

The elegant room filled with refined diners erupted in spontaneous applause, and Spencer raised his hand to accept the well wishes that flowed his way.

"Since I'm going to be busy with Izzy and the baby, I'm going to need an assistant. I looked at the budget, and there's plenty of capital to facilitate a new position."

"I absolutely agree." Chas nodded. "What are you looking for in an assistant?" he asked, stabbing a forkful of arugula.

Spencer thought for a moment. "Veteran. Level-headed. Takes direction well."

Missy and Chas exchanged a look.

"Oh, honey, do I have a candidate for you," Missy said. "There's just one problem. He's in jail."

CHAPTER NINE

The morning after Spencer spilled his big secret, Missy was still basking in the glow that only an about-to-be-new-grandmother knows, but she was also thinking about how she could prove Dodge's innocence so that he could go to work for Spencer and start a new life. She tapped her fingers on her tea cup as she sat curled up on a damask divan pondering her next course of action.

"Okay, in my mind, Shalimar is definitely someone to keep an eye on as a suspect," she began to talk herself through what she knew. "And Penelope may be prissy, but she also seemed to be seriously bitter about Feeney. I think I'll try to set up a lunch with her," Missy mused, reaching for her phone.

"Hey, Penelope, it's Melissa Beckett. I just

wanted to say how great it was seeing you after all these years. I was thinking that we should have lunch sometime and catch up."

"Melissa, hello. Yes, it was lovely seeing you as well. I was planning on going to the club for lunch today. You should join me, if you're free."

"I surely am. What time were you thinking?" Missy asked, her heart pounding. It seemed too easy, but she'd take her chances.

"I like to eat fairly early, before the golfers come in after their morning tee times, so maybe eleven-ish?"

"Eleven works for me. I'll see you there."

Chas entered the parlor just as Missy hung up. "What are you up to now?" he teased, kissing the top of her head.

"I'm so glad you're here. I have a question," Missy said, setting her teacup on the marble top of an antique side table.

"Sure, shoot," Chas replied, sitting beside her.

"I'm having lunch with Penelope at the country club today..." she began.

Chas made a face. "Have fun with that."

"It's for research, but anyway, I can't decide whether to dress to the nines or to play it cool, because I don't know if she's made the reservation in the main dining room or the bistro. What should I do?" Missy asked.

Chas smiled and put a hand on her knee. "You can bridge the gap by wearing something that will be appropriate for either. Since the bistro is usually frequented by the post golf or tennis match crowd, it tends to be a bit more casual, where the dining room is more business casual, as you know. If you wear a simple skirt and sweater, you'll be comfortable in either place."

"Okay, skirt and sweater, got it. Thank you, darlin'" Missy replied, reaching over to kiss his cheek. "I'm going to go get ready."

She chose a brown plaid wool skirt that was mercifully lined with silk, so it didn't make her itch, a chocolate-colored cashmere cowl neck sweater, and a pair of chocolate leather knee-high boots. Her jewelry was simple and elegant because she didn't want to look like she was trying too hard.

She walked into the country club with her head held high and headed to the reception desk.

"Hi, I'm here to meet a friend for lunch," she said.

"Main dining or bistro?" the receptionist asked.

Missy blinked. "I have no idea. Can you look up her name to see if she made a reservation some-where?" she asked.

Before the receptionist could reply, Missy heard a familiar voice.

"Melissa, you look wonderful," Penelope drawled, tucking her arm into Missy's and dragging her down a hallway toward the main dining room. "Who does your work? Do you go to New Orleans for it?" she asked.

"I'm sorry, I don't know what you mean." Missy frowned.

"You know, your face lift, all the little nips and tucks." Penelope chuckled, looking at Missy from head to toe.

"I've never had anything done." Missy shrugged. "I figure I've earned my wrinkles."

Penelope pursed her lips. "Oh please, no one our age looks like that naturally, but if you don't want to reveal your secret surgeon, that's fine."

Missy opened her mouth to speak, but Penelope had dropped her arm and was heading toward someone who had greeted her from another table. It was awkward standing there while Penelope worked the room and Missy had a sneaking suspicion that she was about to have an uncomfortable experience.

Penelope greeted no fewer than ten diners on their way to her reserved table that sat by the windows overlooking the fifth tee. Many of them looked vaguely familiar to Missy, but she couldn't place them.

Once they took their seats, Penelope ordered wine for both of them without asking and stared at Missy. "Okay, Melissa, why don't you tell me why you're really here," she said, without preamble.

It took great effort for Missy not to squirm in her seat. Southern women weren't usually this disturbingly direct.

"After what happened to Feeney, I just wanted to make sure that you were okay," she replied, taking a sip of her wine. It was smooth, mellow, and slightly fruity, and Missy thought that it might go a long way toward making her lunch date much more tolerable.

Penelope's brows rose. "Why wouldn't I be? He was insufferable. I certainly didn't miss him after the divorce and frankly, I'm surprised something like that didn't happen sooner. He always seemed to be angling to cheat people out of their money somehow. Behaved like a starving pauper, though he was far from it." She took a healthy swig of wine and motioned to the sommelier for a refill.

They ordered their lunch and Missy tried again.

"So, you're not even a little sad? You two were together for a long time, right?"

Penelope rolled her eyes. "Depends on how you

define together. He had his little shady business adventures that he kept to himself. I only heard his side of some conversations and drew my own conclusions. I had my shopping and my travels, so I didn't particularly care what he was up to. We slept in the same house and occasionally shared meals or social occasions, but that was about it."

Missy had no idea how to respond to that, but she needn't have worried, Penelope filled the conversation by pointing out different people in the dining room and on the golf course and talking about them. Missy tried hard not to keep glancing at her watch and wondered if they were importing her food from another country because it was taking so long.

At long last, the food arrived. Missy had ordered a lobster roll and a cup of lobster bisque and when it was presented it made her mouth water. Penelope ordered a salad that she mostly moved around on her plate with the tines of her fork.

The lobster was tender, buttery, exquisite and the bisque was a creamy wonder. Missy focused on her food and was enjoying her meal immensely, despite the one-sided conversation. She looked over at Penelope's plate which was still mostly full. Penelope speared one leaf of escarole and chewed it delicately.

"Are you not feeling well?" Missy asked, taking a

sip of wine afterward. She glanced at Penelope's plate again.

"I don't eat," Penelope replied primly. "I firmly believe that there is no way possible to eat and stay fit after a certain age." She gazed pointedly at Missy's already half-empty plate.

"I've always said that half the joy of being from the south is the amazing food." Missy shrugged, tearing a piece of buttered and lightly toasted bread from her lobster roll and dipping it into her bisque. "I'd be a real dragon lady if I didn't eat," Missy said, stifling a grin.

"I take pride in being a dragon lady, so each to their own, I suppose." Penelope's smile seemed a bit forced.

"As long as you're happy with it." Missy chuckled. "Do you have any idea who might have done that awful thing to your ex?" Missy asked.

Penelope sipped her wine and thought for a moment. "Based on his complete lack of people skills, it could have been anyone, but I wouldn't be surprised if it was that gold digging girlfriend of his, or come to think of it, his secretary likely knew enough about him and his business dealings to want him dead. Aside from those two, I'd be looking at the hordes of people he's swindled. The police definitely have their work cut out for them. There are masses of possible suspects," she said with a shrug.

"Who is his secretary?" Missy asked, pretending to be enthralled.

"A plain dumpling of a woman, Patricia Farsley is her name. She's related to him somehow, I think. Why are you so interested anyway?" Penelope speared another leaf of lettuce and stared at Missy.

"I… I was traumatized by the sight of his lifeless body just sprawled out in front of everyone." Missy faked a shudder. "It was an awful thing, no matter who did it or why."

"Death is always ugly, but we shouldn't let it ruin our day when we can't do anything about it," Penelope commented, putting her fork down onto her plate with an air of finality.

"What are you going to do now?" Missy asked.

"Good question. I really don't know. I'm thinking about maybe taking a long cruise in the Caribbean once the weather gets a little colder. Cold air dries my skin out horrifically."

Appalled, Missy tried her best to maintain a neutral expression. "I suppose there's something to be said for getting away from it all."

Penelope nodded and glanced at her phone. "Oh, look at the time. And I haven't even had a chance to ask you all about what it's like living in a haunted house. I have to run, I'm expecting my hairdresser in a few. He flies up from New Orleans, so he gets a bit prickly if I leave him waiting for too long. We'll have to do this again sometime. Lunch is on me, take your time and enjoy," she said, standing and gliding toward the lobby with a breezy wave, leaving Missy staring after her.

Missy relaxed after Penelope's departure and savored every bit of her meal. She thought about having dessert but didn't want to linger too long by herself.

"Thank you so much for coming by today, ma'am. I hope you enjoyed your lunch." The server delicately set the bill down on the table and picked up Missy's empty plate and bowl.

"Oh, excuse me, but I think there's been some sort of mistake. I was Penelope Boggs-Finkleworth's guest, and she said she was going to take care of the bill," Missy said.

The server, seeming flustered, bent down and leaned in. "Listen, you seem really nice, but you're not the first person, and you certainly won't be the last that gets stuck with the bill when Ms. Finklesworth makes an early exit," he confided.

"Oh." Missy's eyes went wide and she dug her

credit card out of her purse and handed it over. A quick glance at the bill nearly made her gasp, but she put a good tip on it to thank the honest server.

On her way out of the dining area, a woman called out to her and beckoned her over.

"Melissa Gladstone, I thought it was you!" she trilled, standing to give Missy a hug.

"Glenda Wayburn? I haven't seen you in decades," Missy replied.

"It's so nice to see you," Glenda said, smiling. "I was just wondering though, what on earth is a nice person like you doing spending time with the likes of Penelope? That woman is not pleasant."

"Her husband died, so I just wanted to make sure she was okay," Missy replied.

"As awful as she is, I know she'd never be the one to murder him," Glenda confided.

"Oh? What makes you say that?"

"Penelope would never do her own dirty work."

Missy nodded, lost in thought, and said her good-byes. She didn't think that Penelope was a suspect either, but she wondered what had gone on in her life that had made her so bitter and cynical.

One mystery at a time. Right now, her goal was to somehow collect clues that would help her spring Santa.

CHAPTER TEN

Pleasantly full and feeling motivated to keep sleuthing, Missy decided on a whim to head over to Feeney Finkelsworth's office. When she opened the glass door, a chime sounded, clearly startling a woman who had her back to the door and was packing items from the reception desk into a box. The rest of the office looked like it had been stripped down to bare bones, aside from a bookcase filled with leather bound books.

"Oh, mercy!" the woman gasped, whirling toward the door, a hand on her chest.

"I'm so sorry. I didn't mean to startle you," Missy said, holding up her hands and giving the woman what she hoped was a reassuring smile.

"Don't worry, it's not your fault. I'm just a bit on

edge, considering what happened," the woman, whom Missy assumed was Patricia, said. She frowned as she gazed at Missy. "I thought I had met most of the board before, but you don't look familiar." She spoke quickly and smoothed her skirt in what looked like a nervous gesture.

"No worries, I'm not a board member. My name is Missy. I just came by to say how sorry I am about Feeney's passing," Missy replied, taking a long look around the office.

"Oh. Well, that's nice of you. I'm Patricia, Feeney's secretary." She stared at Missy with something that looked like suspicion mixed with wonder.

"Nice to meet you, Patricia. It's so empty in here, has the office always been sombare?" Missy asked.

"The police took almost everything in case there might be evidence hidden somewhere." Patricia shrugged.

"Oh, wow. That must've been so scary for you."

"Can't say I was surprised." Patricia's expression landed somewhere between rueful and disgusted.

"Oh?" Missy said, not wanting to throw her off by seeming too interested.

"Yeah. Feeny was my cousin and all, but he was mean to his clients, dishonest with other businesses and just ready to cheat anyone who was innocent enough to fall for it. I know for a fact that there are plenty of people who are mad at him, and rightfully so."

"I'm so sorry. What's going to happen with his company?" Missy asked.

"I have no idea, but I'll be at the reading of his will since I'm the only family member that he spoke to for at least a couple of decades." Patricia shook her head.

"How awful. What happened?"

Patricia fidgeted and pushed up the sleeves of her cardigan. "I won't bore you with details, it's a long story," she finally replied, not quite meeting Missy's eyes.

"Well, if you need to talk, I have plenty of time," Missy said gently.

"That's neighborly of you, but I have to finish packing up my desk, then get back to reconciling our accounts. The police want to know if I come across anything out of the ordinary," Patricia replied, tugging at the hem of her sweater.

"Have you found anything out of the ordinary yet?" Missy asked, knowing full well she was pushing her luck.

"No, ma'am. I've been the bookkeeper here for years and I always put in the data exactly the way that

Feeney gave it to me," she insisted, her jaw jutting forward just a bit.

"Well, it sounds like he was fortunate to have you. Do you have any idea of who could've done such a thing?"

"My money would be on Shalimar." Patricia rolled her eyes. "Everyone knows she had a habit of dating rich older guys, looking for a sugar daddy."

"That's so sad. Was she in his will or something?" Missy asked, glad that Patricia seemed like someone who talked to fill the silence when she was nervous.

"I think he was going to give her everything. I overheard him talking on the phone to the jeweler, asking him to deliver a fake placeholder ring since the real one wasn't ready yet, so I know he was planning to propose at the gala."

"What a tragedy," Missy said, laying the sympathy on thick.

Patricia snorted, then looked as though she was trying to cover up her expression by turning back toward the desk and putting a random coffee mug in the box beside it.

"Well, thanks for stopping by, ma'am, but I really do need to get back to my tasks so that I can have everything done for the police and the board," Patricia said with a shaky smile. She picked up a cup of coffee from the desk and Missy noticed that her hand trembled.

Missy nodded. "I understand. This has to be hard on you though. Are you okay?"

Patricia barked out a humorless laugh. "Yes, ma'am. I'm fine, thanks for asking. I'm just stressed because I have to turn all the accounts over to the board when I'm done going through them and I just want to make sure that I haven't made any mistakes."

"Sure. That's gotta be tough." Missy turned to go but stopped when she reached the door. She turned quickly to say something and noticed that Patricia seemed to be glaring at her.

The expression was so fleeting that Missy wondered if she had actually seen it before it was replaced by a mask of pleasantry.

"Have a nice day, now." Patricia's smile was more frozen than her tone. She gripped the edge of the desk in a white-knuckled manner that was more than unsettling.

Missy left feeling troubled, like maybe she had just been face to face with a killer.

CHAPTER ELEVEN

"You alright?" Spencer asked Missy when he came into the kitchen. "I smelled your gingerbread cupcakes before I opened the door."

"Oh, you know how I am, darlin'." Missy smiled and gave him a hug. "I can't think straight unless I'm elbow deep in flour, butter, and sugar. I'm glad you dropped by. The cupcakes will be cool enough to frost in about half an hour."

"You want me to help?" Spencer chuckled.

"No, honey, I want you to eat. I don't have anyone to distract with them so that I can get more information, and I don't need Chas chain-eating them, so you're going to have to pull your weight in cupcake consumption." Missy grinned.

"It's a dirty job, but somebody has to do it, I

suppose." Spencer sat on a barstool while Missy whipped up the smoothest cream cheese frosting ever. "I did some checking into your Santa today," he said, eyeing one of the still-cooling cupcakes.

"Don't even think about it, mister," Missy warned. "These cupcakes have to have just the right amount of frosting to balance out the spice, so just you hold your horses and tell me what you found out about Santa, er…Dodge," she directed.

"I dug deep, and from everything I can find, he's squeaky clean. Not only does he have no record and no indicators of a drinking problem, back when he was in the military and later an active participant in civilian life, he was involved with charitable organizations and community service. Just an all around good citizen from all accounts. He also has a daughter in Florida. She's an accountant and also a seemingly good citizen."

"Hmm… Sounds like the apple didn't fall far from the tree," Missy commented, thinking.

"Yeah, I seriously doubt that Dodge was involved in Feeney's death," Spencer replied.

"Well, I discovered some interesting things about Feeney today," Missy said, taking out several jars of different kinds of red and green cupcake décor.

"Do tell."

"I went to his office earlier. Not only was it stripped almost entirely bare because the police took everything for evidence, but his secretary was there and she was quite the chatterbox. Turns out that she is his cousin, and she mentioned that there's been some kind of family feud that left her as the only one in Feeney's whole family who still speaks to him."

"That tracks with other things I've seen." Spencer nodded.

"She also tried really hard to lay the blame on his girlfriend, Shalimar," Missy added. "But Patricia was behaving so oddly that I have to wonder if it was her or another family member."

"Shalimar? As in the perfume?" Spencer's brows rose.

Missy chuckled. "Yes, though she'd never heard of it. Honestly, everyone that I've spoken to about Feeney has said that he's a ruthless cheat and swindler, so the possibilities are endless as far as suspects go. But Patricia was very much on edge during our entire conversation and when I turned around as I was about to leave, it looked like she was glaring at me."

"You really need to be careful," Spencer said gently.

"You know me. I'll be just fine. Come to think of

it, Penelope blamed Shalimar too," Missy remembered.

"What does Shalimar do for a living?" Spencer asked.

"She works at a bowling alley, why?"

"I was able to gain access to the autopsy results, and the cause of death was asphyxiation, which doesn't make sense. There were no ligature marks, no foreign body in the throat, no aspirated liquid in the lungs, nothing that would explain how Feeney suffocated to death," Spencer replied.

"So, you're thinking poison," Missy deduced.

Spencer nodded. "I was. But the tox screens came back clean."

"That's strange." Missy frowned. "And just how were you able to gain access to the autopsy results?" she asked, giving him a pointed look.

"I have connections," Spencer replied with an enigmatic smile.

"Of course you do. I'm not even going to ask. So now you're wondering what kinds of poison that Shalimar might have access to?"

"Exactly."

"Her house was really small and really bare, but perfectly clean, so it would make sense that maybe she'd have some cleaning products that would be deadly," Missy mused.

Spencer shook his head. "Unfortunately, no. Cleaning products would've shown up in the tox screen. So would pest control products."

"So, whatever the killer used, they were sneaky about it. Well, that's enough to keep me up at night." Missy sighed. "I still wonder about Patricia. Maybe I should find some excuse to visit her at home."

"Seems to me like gingerbread cupcakes might just be a really good excuse," Spencer pointed out. "But let me put a tracker on your vehicle and phone before you go."

"I'm surprised Chas doesn't have one on the car and my phone already."

"Oh, he does. But mine are more sophisticated, so I'll have more information."

"You boys are lucky I love y'all." Missy shook her head.

"Yes, we are," Spencer agreed with a devilish twinkle in his eye.

CHAPTER TWELVE

With Patricia's address on her phone, Missy set a pink box of festively decorated gingerbread cupcakes on the seat next to her and headed for the outskirts of town. Patricia's house was so far out in the country that Missy was surprised it was in the same parish.

She took a small farm road from the main road that led through town, and it devolved into a dirt road that was thickly treed on both sides with ruts that just looked like they wanted to break an axle.

"Oh geez. Well, if she's a killer and she wants to kill me, they won't find my body for years," Missy muttered, wondering if she should eat a cupcake since it might just be her last meal.

The lumpy, bumpy dirt road went on for miles, until finally, Missy saw a modest ranch home with a line of dog houses along one side and a metal barn on the other. She pulled up as close as she could to the front door and turned the car off, waiting inside for a moment to see if any of the dog houses were occupied by something that might tear her to pieces. When there was no stirring among the dog houses, Missy slowly opened the door, cupcakes in hand, and made her way to the door, scanning the immediate area even as she rang the bell.

A massive mountain of a man dressed in a plaid shirt and overalls opened the door and glared down at her. "You lost?" he said. She could barely see his lips beneath an overgrown beard and mustache.

"Uh…no? At least, I don't think so," Missy replied. "I'm looking for Patricia. I thought she might be feeling a little down, so I brought her some cupcakes."

Patricia appeared at her husband's elbow, frowning.

"How did you find me, and why did you think I'd be feeling down?" she challenged, her face pale, without a trace of makeup, and her hair sloppily tied back in a limp ponytail.

"Because your cousin passed," Missy said gently, her heart thundering in her chest. Suddenly she was quite glad that Spencer had installed advanced equipment on her car and phone. "I brought cupcakes. They're gingerbread. I hope you like gingerbread." She raised the box and offered it to Patricia.

"I like gingerbread," her husband said gruffly, intercepting the box. "Come in."

It sounded more like an order than an offer, but Missy took her opening and followed him inside, not missing the glare that Patricia shot in his direction. She nearly gasped when she saw the interior of the home. Every wall and table featured a menagerie of taxidermies of all species and sizes, with varying degrees of successful preservation. Her stomach bubbled in the back of her throat and she swallowed hard.

"Is hunting your hobby, or taxidermy?" she asked, feigning interest.

Patricia's husband stared at her, half of a cupcake in his massive hand. "Both," he said with a frown, and lumbered off, disappearing down a dim hallway.

"What's your angle?" Patricia asked. "First you stop by the office, now you come all the way out here. Are you some kind of private investigator or something?" She stood, hands on hips, eyes narrowed.

"Oh, uh no. I was just at the event where Feeney passed, and it really had an emotional impact on me. I'm a total stranger. I'd only met him that night, so I can't even imagine what it must be like for you, being family and all," Missy said.

"It didn't have any impact on me." Patricia's tone was like ice.

"Ummm… what?" Missy said, entirely unprepared for that response.

"I really don't care what happened to Feeny. He was a lousy human being and his only love in life was money and swindling. Why would I care about what happened to him?"

"I guess I just didn't see that side of him since I only met him for the first time at the gala," Missy replied, her stomach churning.

"Well then, honey, consider yourself lucky. Since I'm not traveling in gala circles, I'm guessing this will be our last conversation, right?" Patricia gave her a pointed look.

"Yeah, I guess so." Missy nodded. "I'm sorry to have bothered you," she said, edging toward the door.

"Might want to hurry when you step out the door. The dogs usually come back around this time of day," Patricia said, her eyes cold and flat, like those of a shark.

Missy turned on her heel and went out the door, glad that she didn't hear footsteps behind her. She heard a low growl off to her left and didn't bother to turn and look, but sprinted to the car, jumping in and closing the door just as claws clattered against the window right next to her head.

Heart racing, Missy heard growling and snapping as she reversed and turned the car around. The dogs raced alongside her until she was quite a distance down the tree lined road. Her cell phone rang and when she saw Spencer's number on her screen, she picked up.

"You okay?" he asked. "There was a report of impact on your side of the car."

"I'm fine," Missy said, her voice a bit shaky from the gallons of adrenaline pounding through her veins. "It was just a few dogs jumping up."

"Dogs?" Spencer said. "They had to have been pretty sizable. I'm glad that there was a door between you and them."

"Me too, but I'm fine, sugar. I'm headed home."

"Drive safely. I'll be here," Spencer replied before hanging up.

Missy flopped on a chaise in the parlor when she got home. Chas had made her a cup of tea, and it sat on the side table next to a small plate with a chicken sandwich on it.

"So, what happened?" he asked, after kissing her forehead and taking a seat beside her on the chaise.

Spencer sat across the coffee table from them in an antique rocker.

Missy related her experience with Patricia and her husband, and of course the dogs. Both men's faces were grave when she finished. They exchanged a glance.

"What?" Missy said, noticing their expressions.

"How old were the preserved animals that you saw on the walls and tables?" Chas asked.

"Old. They looked… rat chewed." Missy shuddered.

"Would you say they looked like they'd been preserved before the 1980s? Were they that old?" Spencer asked.

"By the looks of those poor critters, yeah, I'd say most of them were older than that. Why?"

Chas took her hand. "Because honey…taxidermy was done using very toxic chemicals like arsenic prior to the 80s. Chances are, if they have those chemicals in their home still, they could have been what was used to poison Feeney."

Missy swallowed. "So, I was just face-to-face with a murderer?" she murmured, dazed and a bit nauseated.

"Quite possibly," Spencer replied. "It's even possible that if the arsenic wasn't still in their home, they could've distilled it out of the carcasses and used it."

"Eww… gross." Missy felt vaguely faint.

"Are you okay, sweetie? You look a little green," Chas asked, his brow furrowed with concern.

"I don't feel very well. Do you think it could be because I was exposed to all of those animals?" Missy asked.

"Doubtful, but not impossible," Spencer replied. "It's more likely the shock of discovering that you may have been in danger. You should have a sip of your tea." He inclined his head toward the steaming cup on the side table.

"Oh, yes, absolutely." Missy nodded, reaching for it. Her hand was surprisingly shaky, but once she'd taken a few sips, she began to feel more like herself.

She reached for her sandwich and took a nibble. "Oh, this is exactly what I need," she said, savoring the bite. "Thank you, honey."

"You're welcome," Chas replied, kissing her cheek.

"I have some things that I need to take care of," Spencer said, rising. "I'm glad you're okay." He moved to the chaise to give Missy a hug and shook Chas's hand. "I'll be back tomorrow. Be safe."

After a deep sleep, Missy arose feeling groggy. She was sitting at the counter drinking coffee and eating a hardboiled egg when the doorbell rang. She got up to answer it and met Chas in the foyer.

"Are you expecting anyone?" he asked.

"No, are you?"

Chas shook his head and they both headed for the door. A seemingly shaken Percy stood in front of them when they opened it.

"Percy, are you okay? What's wrong?" Missy asked as he twisted his cap in his hands. "Please, come in. I'll get you some coffee."

"No ma'am, that wouldn't be proper..." he protested apologetically.

"Nonsense, we make our own rules. Now come on in," Missy insisted.

Percy looked up at Chas, who nodded.

"Okay, ma'am. Thank you kindly."

Missy led him to the kitchen and motioned for him to sit down on a barstool at the island. She got him a cup of coffee and a date and carrot muffin. She and Chas stood on the other side of the island.

"Now, tell us what's wrong," Missy said gently.

"Did y'all not like the holiday decorations?" he asked, looking sad.

"Percy, of course we did. You did such a beautiful job decorating the house. Why would you even ask such a thing?" Missy asked.

"The snowmen, the santa, and every one of them reindeer..." Percy began, then swallowed. "Ma'am, they all been... decapitated."

Missy gasped, her eyes widening. "What?"

"Well, that definitely sends a message," Chas said, his voice grim.

"Don't y'all worry none. I swear I'll redo everything and make it look nice again," Percy promised.

"Thank you, Percy. Please let us know if you find anything else that seems odd," Missy replied.

"Yes'm, I surely will."

Missy changed the subject, asking about his plans for the holidays while he ate his muffin and drank his coffee, then Percy stood to leave. Chas walked him to the door while Missy leaned against the kitchen counter, brooding.

"I'm going to have Spencer beef up our security while he's in town. I'll want motion sensors, security lights, cameras, and a laser perimeter fence," Chas said, coming back into the kitchen.

Missy nodded and shivered, rubbing her upper

arms. "It's escalating. We need to solve this murder fast, because obviously someone knows we're getting close to the truth."

"Too close by the looks of it," Chas added.

"Yeah, clearly. I think I need to make a trip to the bowling alley."

CHAPTER THIRTEEN

"I wonder if Chas has ever been bowling," Missy mused, as she pulled into the parking lot of LaChance's only bowling alley, Lucky Lanes. "We should do that sometime."

She parked among the handful of cars that were there in the early afternoon and headed inside. No sooner had she walked in the door than Shalimar spotted her. She stepped out from behind the shoe rental counter and stared at Missy, eyes narrowed.

"Are you stalking me or what?" she challenged.

"No, not at all. You were just so sick the other day that I wanted to come check on you and make sure you're doing okay. You mentioned you worked here, so here I am. How are you feeling?"

Shalimar shrugged. "I'm fine. I just don't usually eat sugar, so when I scarfed all those cupcakes down, my body rebelled."

"That was probably a good thing." Missy nodded. "I'm glad you're feeling better. Hey, you know… I've never been behind the scenes in a bowling alley; would you mind showing me around if you have time?" she asked.

Shalimar looked around. "We're dead as a door-nail around here right now, so why not. Follow me, you can see how the pin resetting machines work."

Missy really was interested in how the bowling alley functioned and listened intently while Shalimar explained the systems. After the pin resetting and the scoreboard computer, she took Missy behind the shoe counter and went over the process of sterilizing the shoes. Missy wrinkled her nose and Shalimar laughed.

"What's back there?" Missy asked, pointing to a door behind the shoe storage area.

"Just a utility closet. You can look in there if you want to."

Missy moved to the door. "Is it dangerous to breathe in all of those fumes from the shoe spray?" she asked, opening the door.

"Probably, but I'm still alive, so who knows?" Shalimar smirked.

Missy spotted a large metal container of something with a pour spout sitting on the floor against the wall. "What's that?" she asked, nudging it with her toe.

"It's lane oil, and I wouldn't get to close to it if I were you. It's thick and nasty and ruins your clothes if it splashes on them," Shalimar replied.

After they left the shoe area, Shalimar showed Missy the kitchen area.

"Well, there you go. Now you know all of our secrets." Shalimar almost smiled.

"Thanks for the tour, it was fascinating. Listen, I'm glad you're doing better. Take care of yourself," Missy said, heading toward the door.

"If I don't, nobody else will," Shalimar muttered.

Missy immediately looked up shoe sanitizer spray and lane oil when she got back home to her laptop and discovered that, while both could potentially make someone fall ill, neither of them were deadly.

"It has to be Patricia," she muttered, closing the

laptop. "And she made it more than clear that she doesn't want to see me again.

She chewed on her lip, thinking, then brightened. "Unless of course it's to apologize for bothering her."

Before she could change her mind, she boxed up another round of cupcakes and headed for Feeney's office. She had to catch Patricia there because there was no way in the world she was going to walk into her house of taxidermy again. The woods were too dense, the dogs were too big, and the house was too remote for her to take that kind of chance, even if the hulking husband was easily pacified with cupcakes.

Though the front door was unlocked, there didn't seem to be anyone in Feeney's office when Missy went inside. There was a half-filled box of books that had obviously been unloaded from the bookcase that it sat in front of. Curious, Missy went over to look at the ones still left on the shelf. Setting her box of cupcakes on a half empty shelf, she selected a leather-bound copy of Atlas Shrugged and when she opened it, there was a hundred dollar bill in between the pages. She flipped through the book and found several more.

"What do you think you're doing?" Patricia's strident voice made her jump so profoundly, her heart hammering in her chest, that she dropped the book, crisp green bills fluttering to rest around it.

"I'm sorry. I just love books, so I was looking at one, and…"

"Well, hands off. They don't belong to you, and I thought I made it fairly clear that I'm done talking to you," Patricia snapped, entering Missy's space bubble, teeth clenched.

"I…" Missy began, but Patricia stepped closer and interrupted her.

"And before you get any dumb ideas about why the money is here, it's my savings. I can't keep money at home because my husband would spend every dime, not that it's any of your business. You need to just get your nosy little self out of my sight and take your stupid cupcakes with you."

"I'm sorry, I just wanted to apologize and…"

"Save it, society girl. You're in over your head already and you don't have a clue." Patricia made a face and shook her head. "Now take a hike."

Missy bristled. "Look, I was just being nice and trying to help," she said, her southern accent deepening with her ire.

"And I've told you more than once that I don't need or want your help. Now get out before I throw you out." They were nearly nose to nose.

"You don't scare me, even if I know what you're capable of," Missy said, her voice deathly quiet.

"You should be quaking in your designer boots, little miss." Patricia smiled and Missy's blood ran cold, but she didn't give an inch.

"They're ten years old and were a gift, not that it's any of your business," Missy shot back. "I've got my eye on you, Patricia."

"I'm terrified, cupcake lady." Patricia rolled her eyes.

"Then you're way smarter than you seem." Missy smiled sweetly, turned on her heel and forced herself to walk calmly to the door, all the while bracing herself for impact.

None came. This time when she turned the doorknob and looked back at Patricia, there was no mistaking her expression. She was glaring at Missy with pure hatred.

Adrenaline coursing through her veins, Missy continued to walk casually to her car, though she felt anything but relaxed.

Pulling out of the parking lot, she glanced in the rearview mirror but didn't see Patricia.

"Well, that went just great," she said with a sigh. "There's something shady going on with that girl."

As she drove by the bank, Missy spotted Penelope's car, a white Mercedes SUV, and pulled in. When she approached the car, there was a uniformed driver scrolling through social media on his phone, leaning against the door.

"Hi! Are you Penelope's driver?" she asked.

"I sure am. You need a ride, beautiful?" he asked with a mischievous grin.

"No, I'm good, thanks." Missy chuckled. "I was just making sure that this was her car. I'm going to pop in and see her."

"Lucky Penelope," the driver replied.

Penelope was in the lobby on her way out of the bank when Missy walked in.

"Hey girl, you look fabulous!" Missy said. "I'd have to sleep for a week to look that refreshed."

Penelope smiled. "Thank you. It must be my new haircut and the juice cleanse that I did yesterday." She lightly touched her hair, which didn't really look much different than the last time Missy had seen her.

"Juice cleanse? Is that as awful as it sounds?" Missy made a face.

"You get used to it." Penelope shrugged.

"Well, more power to you if it makes you look good and feel good."

"One must do what one must do. A little visit with my aesthetician yesterday didn't hurt either."

"You know, after your comment the other day, I was thinking I might want to at least go get a facial or something before the holidays," Missy replied. "Who do you go to?"

"Aesthetique, over on Shirley Avenue. I'll be going to the reading of Feeney's will at his attorney's office tomorrow at nine o'clock, so I wanted to look extra special even if that awful tart Shalimar is a few decades younger than me and Patricia always looks frumpy. That woman dresses like an old maid and it's a shame, she has potential, I think, to look better."

They headed out of the bank and stood just in front of Penelope's car.

"Well, good luck, I hope there's no drama at the reading. Listen, I saw your car here and came in because I just wanted to let you know that I really enjoyed our conversation at lunch. Maybe we can get together again soon?"

The thought of getting left with the bill at another country club lunch wasn't at all appealing, but Penelope knew enough about Feeney and Patricia that Missy hoped she might be able to help her put the final pieces of the puzzle together.

"Of course. They have complimentary champagne at the club on Tuesdays; we should set something up."

The driver opened the door and let Penelope in, winking at Missy as she walked by. She smiled and waved.

"Well, well, well… Looks like I'll be on a stakeout tomorrow," Missy murmured to herself.

CHAPTER FOURTEEN

Missy parked under a giant oak tree on a street that ran alongside Feeney's attorney's office at eight-thirty, so that she'd be there well ahead of the reading of the will. Coffee in hand, she leaned back in her seat, her eyes on the parking lot behind the office building. She had a great view but was hidden by the landscaping of the house immediately across from the entrance.

Shalimar was the first to arrive. She stepped out of a city bus halfway down the block from where Missy was parked. Missy's jaw dropped when she saw her. In full makeup, with her hair a silken mass of golden perfection, she wore a pink tweed Chanel suit under a Burberry trench coat and carried a coordinating Hermes purse.

"Wow, if that's the kind of clothing that Feeney bought her, no wonder she was upset about a fake diamond ring," Missy mused.

While Shalimar stopped on the sidewalk by the parking lot and checked her makeup in a purse mirror, Penelope's SUV and Patricia's nondescript compact car pulled in.

Penelope, helped from the car by her driver, was dressed in winter ivory from head to toe and looked like she'd just stepped away from a photo shoot for Senior Vogue. Patricia, who got out of the car next to her, looked dowdy in a drab, grey, ill-fitting pantsuit. The two women greeted each other, and Missy could see the tension in their posture and movements even from where she sat.

Shalimar stashed her mirror in her purse and spoke to them. Patricia nodded, but Penelope breezed past as though she hadn't even seen her.

Shalimar speed walked past them, no mean feat in stilettos, and was the first one in the door, yanking it open and leaving it to slam shut on the women behind her. Patricia opened it and gestured for Penelope to go through, which she did, head held high.

Missy took a sip of her coffee and noticed that Penelope's driver was reading a magazine behind the wheel while the SUV idled, puffing thin clouds of white from its exhaust. Patricia's husband waited in the car in the attorney's parking lot, his head back against the seat, looking as though he might be snoring.

"I wonder how long this is going to take," Missy muttered, nibbling on a piece of Cajun dried mango that she'd brought with her.

She tried to distract herself by reading the news on her phone but couldn't manage to keep an eye on the door and still pay attention to the article she was trying to read, so she stashed her phone in her purse and finished her now-cold coffee while she waited.

After only half an hour, Patricia stormed out of the building, slamming the door behind her, and practically threw herself into the passenger seat of her car.

Shalimar came out next, red faced and crying. She strode down the street as though the hounds of Hades were after her, holding her thin jacket closed with crossed arms, head down.

Penelope strolled out of the office last, looking like the cat that ate the canary. When her driver came around to open the door for her, she said something, put her hand on his arm and laughed before getting into the car. He lifted the edge of her white mink trimmed coat, keeping it from resting in the door frame, and closed the door.

"Do I, or do I not?" Missy mused, watching Shalimar flounce down the sidewalk in her rearview mirror. She sighed. "Fine, I will."

Watching for traffic, she made a U-turn in the street and pulled alongside the still-crying young woman.

"Shalimar? Are you okay?" she called out, lowering the window on the passenger side.

"No, leave me alone," she snapped, her voice clouded with tears.

"Why don't you let me give you a ride somewhere, it's too cold to be out here walking," Missy insisted.

Shalimar stopped and stared at her, wiping tears away. "Fine."

She got into the car and pulled a tissue out of her purse.

"What's wrong, darlin'," Missy asked, after Shalimar had a moment to regain her composure.

"I really thought he loved me," she whispered, tears welling again. "But I guess he didn't care at all."

"Feeney, you mean? Why do you say that? I'm sure he cared about you."

"He has a funny way of showing it. I was just at the reading of his will. He left his evil secretary a bookcase with books full of money that he stashed there because he was paranoid about banks, I got a measly little life insurance check, and that wicked old witch of the south, Penelope, got everything else. I mean, seriously, who leaves their whole estate to their ex?" Shalimar pouted. "I knew she was trying to get back with him when they had that drink together at the gala. She couldn't stand seeing me happy and with all of his money. I can't believe he didn't change the will. She must've come in and put him under a spell with some kind of voodoo."

"You sound pretty mad," Missy observed.

"I *am* mad," Shalimar said shrilly. "If I would've had more time with Feeney before his secretary killed him, I would have been left with everything instead of that old hag."

Missy's brows rose and her heart sped up. "You think Patricia killed him?"

"I'd almost swear to it. You should have heard how she screeched when she found out that I got something and Penelope got almost all the rest. Screamed something about keeping his cousins from killing him and maybe she shouldn't have. Now I wonder if she's going to come after me and the ex, she was so nasty."

"Money does strange things to people some-times," Missy said.

"Or lack of it. As far as I know, Patricia was flat broke, but she made it sound like Feeney owed her for some reason."

Missy nodded, content to let Shalimar's mouth continue to run.

"And then the smarmy ex had the nerve to say that she's leaving for the Caribbean."

"Oh really?" Missy said. "When is she doing that?"

"Tomorrow."

CHAPTER FIFTEEN

Missy gazed at her sterile, but cheery, surroundings, her stomach churning. A young, handsome doctor came in and greeted her.

"Good morning, Mrs. Beckett. I'm Dr. Bensen, and I'll be working with you today."

"It's nice to meet you," Missy replied. "Thanks for fitting me in."

"It's our pleasure," he said with a smile. "Any friend of Penelope's is a friend of ours."

"Your best customer?" Missy joked.

"Pretty close." Dr. Bensen chuckled. "Now, what can I do for you today?"

"Well, I was thinking… I have this sort of deep wrinkle right between my eyebrows that I'd like to make go away. Is there anything that you can do about that?" Missy pointed to the spot that had plagued her for years.

"Absolutely. We can give you a Botox treatment that will allow those muscles to relax and ease back into the proper shape." The doctor touched the area lightly, depressing his fingers a bit.

"Oh, that would be great, thank you. I think other than that, maybe just a nice hydrating facial," Missy nodded.

"Perfect. I'll have to ask you to step out into the hall with Nurse Nancy while I prepare for your treatment. Then, we'll get you all taken care of, just in time for the holidays."

Missy stared blankly at him for a moment.

"Come with me, Mrs. Beckett," Nancy said, gesturing toward the door.

"Oh, okay." Missy followed her into the hall, and Nancy closed the door behind them. "So, why do we have to come out here?" she asked, mystified.

"So that Dr. Bensen can access the Botox medication," the nurse replied.

"Is it a secret recipe or something?" Missy chuckled.

"No, but, confidentially, one of our full syringes went missing very recently and now it's just policy to not open the refrigerator when patients are in the room," Nancy said in a low voice.

"Wait, did you say syringes?" Missy asked, widening her eyes.

"Well, yes. Why?"

"As in needles?" Missy swayed a bit.

"That's how the treatment is given, yes. Are you okay?" the nurse asked, putting a hand out to steady her."

"No, I'm definitely not okay, and I'm definitely not getting a shot between my eyebrows. I'd pass right out. Sorry, but I have to go," Missy said, moving quickly toward the exit.

"We can still do your facial," Nancy called after her.

Missy didn't even turn around.

Sprinting from the doctor's office, Missy got in the car and placed a call to Chas, then headed to Penelope's house.

She pulled up to the tall iron gates that surrounded Penelope's huge chateau and pushed the button on the wrought iron post on the left side of the driveway.

A man's voice answered, asking her to state her

business.

"Oh, I don't have any business, I'm just Penelope's friend Missy Beckett," Missy replied, injecting a heavy dose of cheer into her tone.

"One moment," the humorless voice responded.

Missy sat, her pulse racing, for what seemed like forever, until finally the gates unlocked with a loud metallic clang and slid slowly to the sides to allow her through. She drove through a column of sculpted trees that lined the long driveway to the house, and pulled into the circular drive, where a man in a black suit stood, apparently waiting for her.

"Melissa Beckett, I presume," he said, after opening her door for her.

"Yep, that's me," Missy replied, amused at his formality. "And you are?"

"The House Manager," was the clipped reply.

"That's a funny name," Missy teased, determined to make the icy gent smile.

"Follow me, please," he replied, striding toward the soaring double doors.

"Aye-aye, sir," Missy muttered under her breath, giving in to the futility of extracting a human response from him.

If he heard her, he gave no indication. He opened the door and gestured for her to enter.

"Wow, that's a lot of marble," Missy observed, gazing at the formal foyer.

"This way, please," the house manager continued on, leading her to a gigantic living room with a fireplace that she could've easily stood up in. "Mrs. Finklesworth will be with you momentarily," he said, leaving her standing alone in the cavernous room. Fortunately, she wasn't alone long.

"Melissa, lovely to see you, even if your timing is quite possibly the worst. I'm packing up to leave for the Caribbean. What do you need?" Penelope said, smiling a smile that didn't quite reach her eyes.

"Oh, I'm sorry. You didn't mention it when I saw you yesterday. I guess our champagne Tuesday date at the club will have to wait, huh?" Missy said.

"Oh, right. Yes, it will, but surely you didn't come all the way over here to ask me that," Penelope prompted, making a pointed glance at the slim Rolex on her wrist.

"No, you're right, I didn't. I have an odd question, actually," Missy began.

"Well, come on, out with it," Penelope directed, brows raised.

"You were such a vision at the gala. I fell absolutely in love with your dress. Chas and I have a function next month, and I wanted to have some aspects of my dress mirror the one you were wearing. I was hoping, if you have it back from the cleaners, that I might be able to take a look and maybe some photos. I mean, I'll have to compensate for the fact that my hips aren't as slim as yours, but I think that can be done tastefully," Missy replied.

"Can this wait until I get back?" Penelope sighed.

"That depends. When will you get back?"

"Probably six or seven weeks from now." Penelope shrugged.

Missy shook her head. "Oh no, that wouldn't give me enough time to have a dress made before the event."

"I can give you the name of my designer," Penelope offered.

"I only work with my person," Missy replied ruefully. "It'll just take a few seconds. I'll go look at the gown, snap a couple of pictures, and be out of your hair in a flash, I promise," she said, crossing her heart with a grin.

"Fine. Come with me. Can you survive a double flight of stairs, or do you need the elevator?"

Missy miraculously didn't let her irritation show. "I'm the same age you are, Penelope, and quite capable of keeping up." She pasted on a smile.

"Good. Get hopping then," Penelope ordered,

striding purposefully from the room, with Missy by her side.

The grand staircase leading to Penelope's bedroom suite was massive, occupying the center of the chateau and surrounded by balconies on either side. Penelope's room was huge as well and draped in cream-colored velvet and satin.

"Wow, this is beautiful," Missy remarked.

"It's getting redone in the spring," Penelope replied, moving toward a panel in the wall. She touched it lightly and it opened into a custom closet that was more spacious than many living rooms. It had a divan, a center island that was lit and mirrored, and more clothing and shoe racks than Missy had ever seen in one place.

Penelope's gowns hung in garment bags at the end of the closet, and she quickly flipped through them until she found the one she'd worn to the gala.

"Here," she said, thrusting the hanger toward Missy. "You can take it out and lay it on the bed. Get your pictures and you can show yourself out, if you don't mind. I'll be in the closet selecting my accessories for the trip."

"Sure, I can do that," Missy agreed, taking the gown and heading toward the tall king-sized bed.

She took it carefully out of the bag, took several

photos, and carefully placed the garment bag back over it. She took it to the closet and hung it back on the rack.

"Thanks a million, and have a great trip," she called out, as she passed by Penelope, who was organizing her jewelry.

"You can call me when I get back," Penelope replied absently, holding up two necklaces and studying them.

"Will do," Missy said, feeling as though a weight had been lifted from her shoulders.

She held on to the solid marble banister and trotted quickly down to the ground floor, hurrying toward the door.

"Thank goodness for gravity," she muttered. The trip downstairs had been much easier than going up had been.

The house manager appeared out of nowhere when her feet hit the foyer floor, and he opened the front door for her.

"Thanks. Great meeting you." She smiled.

"Have a lovely day, madame," he droned, clearly not meaning a word of it.

"Oh, I will." Missy caught his eye and grinned.

He gazed back at her with a speculative look, his eyes shrewd.

CHAPTER SIXTEEN

"I need to see Detective Cahill immediately," Missy said, staring down the desk sergeant.

"I'll see if he's available," the fireplug of a woman drawled.

"If he doesn't come out here to see me, I'm going to vault right over this counter. I know where his office is. Ask him if he wants to bust a murderer or not," Missy ordered.

The sergeant stared at her. "Wait here," she said, eyes narrowed.

"I'll wait, but I promise you, I'm not going to wait long," Missy warned.

In a matter of minutes, the sergeant re-appeared with a rather cranky-looking Detective Cahill behind her.

"I should have guessed," he said when he saw Missy. "Come on back."

The sergeant opened the barrier between the lobby and the offices, and Missy followed Cahill back to his inner sanctum.

"What's your issue with our department today?" he asked, his tone dripping sarcasm and conde-scension.

"You have an innocent man sitting in your jail, and I know who the real murderer is," Missy replied.

Cahill sighed and leaned back in his chair. "I'm all ears," he said with less enthusiasm than one would use when confirming a colonoscopy.

"Did you happen to find a piece of fabric snagged on the stairs when Feeney Finklesworth's body was found?" Missy asked.

The detective quirked an eyebrow. "And just how did you know about that?"

Missy pulled out her phone. "Because I took a photo of it when the body was discovered and you shooed me away from the scene. Look at the date and time stamp." She showed him her phone and his eyes narrowed.

"Go on."

Missy flipped through her photos until she came to the ones that she took at Penelope's chateau earlier.

"This is the dress. Here's where the fabric was torn, and here's the blood spatter on the hem of the sleeve that likely happened after Penelope Finklesworth whacked Dodge over the head. He had to have been seated on the steps to get some air when Feeney came out, fell down the steps, and died, so she hit him and ran."

Cahill looked skeptical. "Which would make perfect sense if Feeney had died from blunt force trauma during a fall, but he didn't." He leaned forward, resting his forearms on the desk.

"No, of course he didn't. At that point he wasn't thinking straight because he probably couldn't breathe," Missy said.

Something flickered across Cahill's expression for a moment. "Why would you think he couldn't breathe?" he asked slowly, his eyes boring into hers.

"Because Penelope didn't kill him by pushing him down the stairs. She had a drink with him that night, when she got to the gala, and I'd bet you dollars to donuts that she put Botox solution into his drink." Missy stared right back.

Cahill made a face. "And just how would she have come to possess Botox solution?"

"When I talked to her doctor, the nurse told me that they'd changed their office protocols because a vial of it had disappeared recently. Penelope had gone to get some procedures the day before the gala."

Cahill seemed to be digesting the information.

"And what possible motive would she have had?" he asked. "She was already a wealthy woman. She did well in the divorce."

"Yeah, she did, but she also knew that Feeney was going to propose to his fiancée that night and make Shalimar his beneficiary."

"How do you know that his fiancée wasn't his beneficiary?" Cahill stared down at his desk, tapping his fingers as he seemed to be thinking through what Missy had presented.

"Because I ran into her after the reading of the will. She and Feeney's secretary received a pittance, and Penelope was awarded the vast majority of his estate."

Cahill swallowed, then was silent for a moment. "You know you're treading very near an interference charge," he said quietly.

"Whatever," Missy shot back immediately. "If you want to catch your killer, you might want to hurry, because she's on her way to the airport to leave for the Caribbean."

CHAPTER SEVENTEEN

Missy and Chas cuddled together on the sofa, wearing their Christmas sweaters, sipping cocoa, and gazing at the beautifully lit tree, while carols played softly in the background. The living room was resplendent with garland, ornaments, and brightly colored gifts under the tree.

"You ready for tonight?" Chas asked, kissing her temple.

"I can't wait for tonight." Missy grinned. "You know I'm just a big kid when it comes to the holidays."

"I love that about you," Chas murmured into her hair. "And you're also tricky."

"Tricky? Who, me?" Missy feigned innocence.

"You knew that Dodge would come to Christmas

Eve dinner if you told him that you wanted him to play Santa," Chas replied.

"Absolutely. I just hated the thought of him sitting at the boarding house by himself on Christmas Eve when we're having a wonderful dinner." Missy shrugged.

"I'm sure Gracie would've fed him a good meal, but I agree. I'm glad he's coming over, and that you invited Percy and his wife too."

"That took some convincing."

"It's worth the effort."

Missy nodded. "Totally worth it."

They set their empty cocoa mugs on the coffee table and enjoyed the golden silence between them, feeling so warm and cozy that they eventually drifted off to sleep.

Missy jolted awake and sat bolt upright. "Oh no!" she exclaimed. "What time is it?"

She grabbed for her phone as Chas sat up, yawning. "I feel great," he said.

"That's good because we need to get upstairs and get ready. Percy, Kaylee, and Dodge will be here before we know it!" Missy replied, clambering up from the sofa and dashing upstairs. "Come on now, no time to dilly dally," she called out.

She jogged up the stairs and darted into her closet,

putting on the red velvet cocktail dress that she'd bought for the occasion.

"Hey honey, can you come in here and zip me up?" she called out.

"Be right there," she heard Chas answer from his closet.

When he walked in the door, it nearly took Missy's breath away. He looked so handsome in his black suit with a red snowflake tie that she felt a tinge of color rising in her cheeks.

"How on earth did I get to marry the most amazing man on the planet?" she asked, her heart full.

"Strategic capture and containment on my part," Chas teased.

"Well, thank you for that, mister," she said, turning so that he could zip up her dress.

"You look beautiful," Chas said softly, turning her around to face him after he zipped up her dress.

"Oh, darlin', you ain't seen nothing yet. Now scoot on out so I can finish getting ready. The caterer should be here any second." She shooed him playfully away.

"I can't believe you're having company and not cooking," Chas said, heading out.

"Sometimes it's better to focus on people rather

than prep work," Missy replied, sitting down at her vanity to do her hair and makeup.

"Gorgeous and wise too. I'm a lucky man," Chas replied from somewhere in their room.

Missy looked in the mirror and smiled.

The candlelit table was set, and servers stood by for the guests to arrive.

Missy jumped when the doorbell rang. She grabbed Chas by the arm and practically dragged him to the foyer. Dodge was the first to arrive so that he could get set up as Santa when Percy arrived with his wife and granddaughters.

"It's so good to see you, Dodge," Missy said, giving him a hug when he came in. Chas shook his hand.

"You have to be the most convincing Santa I've ever seen," he said.

"I'll take that as a compliment, sir," Dodge said with a shy smile.

"It definitely is. Let me show you where we set up your Santa chair. These little girls are going to be delighted to see you," Chas replied, leading him to the living room while Missy went to the kitchen to take a sip of wine.

They chatted with Dodge in the living room, enjoying easy conversation.

"I wanted to thank you, Missy, for convincing the police that I didn't belong in jail," Dodge said, his tone warm.

"You're more than welcome. I can't stand to see injustice, particularly when it involves someone who's so nice as well as innocent."

"Let's get this party started," Missy heard from behind her left shoulder and turned to see Kaylee come into the living room wearing a green silk dress.

"Honey, you look amazing," Missy said, jumping up to hug her daughter. Chas did the same and Kaylee introduced herself to Dodge, telling him she hoped she was on the 'nice' list.

He laughed and said that he was sure she was and Kaylee, with eyes sparkling, said, "Oh, Mom, I brought you an early Christmas present, let me go get it. I'll be right back."

"You didn't have to do that," Missy called after her as she strode back toward the kitchen.

After a few moments, Kaylee called out, "Okay, Mom, Dad, close your eyes."

"Got it," Chas replied.

Missy heard some shuffling and then Kaylee said, "Open them."

Missy opened her eyes and they immediately flooded with tears. "Charlie!" she exclaimed, dashing to her son, only to be wrapped up in a bear hug. "You said you couldn't make it home for Christmas. I'm so glad you came, darlin'," she said, wiping her eyes when Charlie set her down so that he could hug Chas.

"I finished my finals, called off from work, and here I am," Charlie replied with a mischievous grin.

Just as Missy was about to reply, the doorbell rang.

"Oh, that must be Percy and family," Missy said, clapping her hands together in excitement and heading for the door.

"Some things never change," Kaylee said, exchanging a glance with Charlie and gazing fondly at her mother before she followed her to the foyer.

"Merry Christmas!" Missy said, when she opened the door to let in Percy, his wife, and his two grand-daughters, Chantal and Samara. They were a year apart in age, at 8 and 9, but were dressed identically in soft pink taffeta dresses that had sparkly chiffon skirts.

"Girls, you look amazing and I have a surprise for you," Missy said, taking each of them by the hand while Kaylee led Percy and his wife to the living room.

"Santa!" they cried out in unison, running to Dodge, whose eyes positively sparkled.

"Ho, ho, ho!! Chantal and Samara, how are you tonight?" he boomed.

The sisters looked at each other with amazement.

"He knows us," Samara whispered, wide-eyed.

"Of course I know you," Dodge said, ever the perfect Santa. "And I know that you've been good girls this year."

Tears sprung to Missy's eyes, and the doorbell rang again. She gave Chas a mystified look.

"Were you expecting anyone else?" she asked.

He merely shrugged, smiled, and said, "Let's go see who's ringing our bell on Christmas Eve."

He took her hand and led her to the foyer.

"Chas Beckett, what are you up to?" she asked.

"Who me?" he said with a mischievous grin.

He opened the door and Spencer stood on the porch, carrying a present.

"Spencer, honey! I thought you went home to your beautiful wife," Missy exclaimed, her eyes welling.

"I did," he replied, stepping to the side.

"Izzy!!" Missy didn't hold back the tears as she

sprang forward to lead Izzy into the house for a long hug. "Oh sweetie, I'm so glad to see you! Should you be traveling in your condition? Do you need to sit down?"

Izzy laughed. "I'm fine, it's early enough to travel without worrying about it. I missed you so much," she said, wiping at her eyes.

"Oh honey, I missed you too. Thank you for coming to see us," Missy said, wrapping an arm around Izzy as they went back to the living room and introduced everyone.

Dodge had given the girls presents to unwrap and they were busily playing with new toys while the adults talked.

"If y'all are hungry, we can head to the dining room," Missy announced, and the doorbell rang again.

"I'll get it," Spencer volunteered.

"I have no idea who it could be," Missy commented.

Then they all heard voices raised in song.

"Carolers!" Kaylee said. "I love that! Let's all go see them."

Chas opened both of the double doors so that everyone could see the carolers as they sang. The beautiful notes of Silent Night held them spellbound, and as the last note faded away, a woman who had been standing in the back, her hat pulled down low and her scarf covering her chin, stepped forward.

Staring at Dodge, her eyes glimmering with tears, she said, "Merry Christmas, Daddy."

A sob choking in his throat, Dodge stepped forward to embrace his daughter for the first time in more than a decade.

There wasn't a dry eye anywhere. Chas squeezed Missy's hand, then brought it to his lips and kissed it. "Guess I'm not the only one who knows how to plan a surprise," he whispered.

Missy grinned.

"Whoa! Santa has a daughter?" Chantal said, her eyes like saucers.

Everyone laughed, as Dodge wiped his eyes.

"Yes Chantal, even Santa has a daughter," he said, his voice husky with emotion.

"I don't know about y'all, but I'm hungry. Let's eat," Missy said, drawing laughter from the crowd.

"Yeah, let's eat," Dodge said, taking his daughter's hand and leading her into the house.

As they passed Missy, he stopped and hugged her. "I don't know what I did to deserve a friend like you, but I'm grateful," he said.

"Me too," Missy replied.

"So, Dodge…" Spencer came and clapped him on the back. "Have I got a deal for you. Are you familiar with Beckett Enterprises?" he asked, walking alongside Santa and his daughter.

"I've heard of it."

"You're going to hear a lot more of it." Spencer grinned.

Missy and Chas hung back as the carolers moved on to the next house, watching the joy in their guests' faces as they headed into the dining room.

"Best Christmas ever?" Chas said, wrapping his arm around his beloved wife.

"Hands down. Until next year." Missy smiled.

"Next year?" Chas's brows rose.

"Spencer and Izzy are going to have a little one coming to see Santa. We need to start preparing now."

"One beautiful Christmas at a time, okay sweetie?" Chas laughed.

"Deal," Missy said, standing on tiptoe to give him a kiss.

AUTHOR'S NOTE

I'd love to hear your thoughts on my books, the storylines, and anything else that you'd like to comment on—reader feedback is very important to me. My contact information, along with some other helpful links, is listed on the next page. If you'd like to be on my list of "folks to contact" with updates, release and sales notifications, etc.… just shoot me an email and let me know. Thanks for reading!

Also…

… if you're looking for more great reads, Summer Prescott Books publishes several popular series by outstanding Cozy Mystery authors.

CONTACT SUMMER PRESCOTT BOOKS PUBLISHING

Blog and Book Catalog: http://summerprescottbooks.com
Email: summer.prescott.cozies@gmail.com

And…be sure to check out the Summer Prescott Cozy Mysteries fan page and Summer Prescott Books Publishing Page on Facebook – let's be friends!

To sign up for our fun and exciting newsletter, which will give you opportunities to win prizes and swag, enter contests, and be the first to know about New Releases, click here: http://summerprescottbooks.com

Manufactured by Amazon.ca
Bolton, ON

53678456R00081